Pippi Longstocking

Pippi Longstocking

ASTRID LINDGREN

TRANSLATED FROM THE SWEDISH BY FLORENCE LAMBORN

ILLUSTRATED BY LOUIS S. GLANZMAN

The Viking Press · New York

Copyright 1950 by The Viking Press, Inc.
All rights reserved
Viking Seafarer edition
Issued in 1969 by The Viking Press, Inc.
625 Madison Avenue, New York, N.Y. 10022
Library of Congress catalog card number: 50-10396
Fic 1. Sweden
Printed in U.S.A.

CONTENTS

ILLUSTRATIONS

Pippi Longstocking

1.
Pippi Moves into Villa Villekulla

Way out at the end of a tiny little town was an old overgrown garden, and in the garden was an old house, and in the house lived Pippi Longstocking. She was nine years old, and she lived there all alone. She had no mother and no father, and that was of course very nice because there was no one to tell her to go to bed just when she was having the most fun, and no one who could make her take cod liver oil when she much preferred caramel candy.

Once upon a time Pippi had had a father of whom she was extremely fond. Naturally she had had a mother too, but that was so long ago that Pippi didn't remember her at all. Her mother had died when Pippi was just a tiny baby and lay in a cradle and howled so that nobody could go anywhere near her. Pippi was sure that her mother was now up in Heaven, watching her little girl through a peephole in the sky, and Pippi often waved up at her and called, "Don't you worry about me. I'll always come out on top."

Her father Pippi had not forgotten. He was a sea captain who sailed on the great ocean, and Pippi had sailed with him in his ship until one day her father blew overboard in a storm and disappeared. But Pippi was absolutely certain that he would come back. She would never believe that he had drowned; she was sure he had floated until he landed on an island inhabited by cannibals. And she thought he had become the king of all the cannibals and went around with a golden crown on his head all day long.

"My papa is a cannibal king; it certainly isn't every child who has such a stylish papa," Pippi used to say with satisfaction. "And as soon as my papa has built himself a boat he will come and get me, and I'll be a cannibal princess. Heigh-ho, won't that be exciting?"

Her father had bought the old house in the garden many years ago. He thought he would live there with Pippi when he grew old and couldn't sail the seas any longer. And then this annoying thing had to happen, that he blew into the ocean, and while Pippi was waiting for him to come back she went straight home to Villa Villekulla. That was the name of the house. It stood there ready and waiting for her. One lovely summer evening she had said good-by to all the sailors on her father's boat. They were all so fond of Pippi, and she of them.

"So long, boys," she said and kissed each one on the forehead. "Don't you worry about me. I'll always come out on top."

Two things she took with her from the ship: a little monkey whose name was Mr. Nilsson—he was a present from her father—and a big suitcase full of gold pieces. The sailors stood up on the deck and watched as long as they could see her. She walked straight ahead without looking back at all, with Mr. Nilsson on her shoulder and her suitcase in her hand.

"A remarkable child," said one of the sailors as Pippi disappeared in the distance.

He was right. Pippi was indeed a remarkable child. The most remarkable thing about her was that she was so strong. She was so very strong that in the whole wide world there was not a single police officer who was as strong as she. Why, she could lift a whole horse if she wanted to! And she wanted to. She had a horse of her own that she had bought with one of her many gold pieces the day she came home to Villa Villekulla. She had always longed for a horse, and now here he was living on the porch. When Pippi wanted to drink her afternoon coffee there, she simply lifted him down into the garden.

Beside Villa Villekulla was another garden and another house. In that house lived a father and mother and two charming children, a boy and a girl. The boy's name was Tommy and the girl's Annika. They were good, well brought up, and obedient children. Tommy would never think of biting his nails, and he always did exactly what his mother told him to do. Annika never fussed when she didn't get her own way, and she always looked so pretty in her little well-ironed cotton dresses; she took the greatest care not to get them dirty. Tommy and Annika played nicely with each other in their garden, but they had often wished for a playmate. While Pippi was still sailing on the ocean with her father, they often used to hang over the fence and say to each other, "Isn't it silly that nobody ever moves into that house. Somebody ought to live there—somebody with children."

On that lovely summer evening when Pippi for

the first time stepped over the threshold of Villa Villekulla, Tommy and Annika were not at home. They had gone to visit their grandmother for a week; and so they had no idea that anybody had moved into the house next door. On the first day after they came home again they stood by the gate, looking out onto the street, and even then they didn't know that there actually was a playmate so near. Just as they were standing there considering what they should do and wondering whether anything exciting was likely to happen or whether it was going to be one of those dull days when they couldn't think of anything to play—just then the gate of Villa Villekulla opened and a little girl stepped out. She was the most re-markable girl Tommy and Annika had ever seen. She was Miss Pippi Longstocking out for her morn-ing promenade. This is the way she looked:

Her hair, the color of a carrot, was braided in two tight braids that stuck straight out. Her nose was the shape of a very small potato and was dotted all over with freckles. It must be admitted that the mouth under this nose was a very wide one, with strong white teeth. Her dress was rather unusual. Pippi herself had made it. She had meant it to be blue, but there wasn't quite enough blue cloth, so Pippi had sewed little red pieces on it here and there. On her long thin legs she wore a pair of long stockings, one brown and the other black; and she had on a pair of black shoes that were exactly twice as long as her feet. These shoes her father had bought for her in South America so that Pippi should have something to grow into, and she never wanted to wear any others.

But the thing that made Tommy and Annika open their eyes widest of all was the monkey sitting on the strange girl's shoulder. It was a little monkey, dressed in blue pants, yellow jacket, and a white straw hat.

Pippi walked along the street with one foot on the sidewalk and the other in the gutter. Tommy and Annika watched as long as they could see her. In a little while she came back, and now she was walking backward. That was because she didn't want to turn around to get home. When she reached Tommy's and Annika's gate she stopped.

The children looked at each other in silence. At last Tommy spoke. "Why did you walk backward?"

"Why did I walk backward?" said Pippi. "Isn't this a free country? Can't a person walk any way he wants to? For that matter, let me tell you that in

Egypt everybody walks that way, and nobody thinks it's the least bit strange."

"How do you know?" asked Tommy. "You've never been in Egypt, have you?"

"I've never been in Egypt? Indeed I have. That's one thing you can be sure of. I have been all over the world and seen many things stranger than people walking backward. I wonder what you would have said if I had come along walking on my hands the way they do in Farthest India."

"Now you must be lying," said Tommy.

Pippi thought a moment. "You're right," she said sadly, "I am lying."

"It's wicked to lie," said Annika, who had at last gathered up enough courage to speak.

"Yes, it's very wicked to lie," said Pippi even more sadly. "But I forget it now and then. And how can you expect a little child whose mother is an angel and whose father is king of a cannibal island and who herself has sailed on the ocean all her life—how can you expect her to tell the truth always? And for that matter," she continued, her whole freckled face lighting up, "let me tell you that in the Belgian Congo there is not a single person who tells the truth. They lie all day long. Begin at seven in the morning and

keep on until sundown. So if I should happen to lie
now and then, you must try to excuse me and to remember that it is only because I stayed in the Belgian Congo a little too long. We can be friends anyway, can't we?"

"Oh, sure," said Tommy and realized suddenly
that this was not going to be one of those dull days.

"By the way, why couldn't you come and have
breakfast with me?" asked Pippi.

"Why not?" said Tommy. "Come on, let's go."

"Oh, yes, let's," said Annika.

"But first I must introduce you to Mr. Nilsson,"
said Pippi, and the little monkey took off his cap
and bowed politely.

Then they all went in through Villa Villekulla's
tumbledown garden gate, along the gravel path,
bordered with old moss-covered trees—really good
climbing trees they seemed to be—up to the house,
and on to the porch. There stood the horse, munch-
ing oats out of a soup bowl.

"Why do you have a horse on the porch?" asked
Tommy. All horses he knew lived in stables.

"Well," said Pippi thoughtfully, "he'd be in the
way in the kitchen, and he doesn't like the parlor."

Tommy and Annika patted the horse and then

went on into the house. It had a kitchen, a parlor, and a bedroom. But it certainly looked as if Pippi had forgotten to do her Friday cleaning that week. Tommy and Annika looked around cautiously just in case the King of the Cannibal Isles might be sitting in a corner somewhere. They had never seen a cannibal king in all their lives. But there was no father to be seen, nor any mother either.

Annika said anxiously, "Do you live here all alone?"

"Of course not!" said Pippi. "Mr. Nilsson and the horse live here too."

"Yes, but I mean, don't you have any mother or father here?"

"No, not the least little tiny bit of a one," said Pippi happily.

"But who tells you when to go to bed at night and things like that?" asked Annika.

"I tell myself," said Pippi. "First I tell myself in a nice friendly way; and then, if I don't mind, I tell myself again more sharply; and if I still don't mind, then I'm in for a spanking—see?"

Tommy and Annika didn't see at all, but they thought maybe it was a good way. Meanwhile they had come out into the kitchen and Pippi cried,

> *"Now we're going to make a pancake,*
> *Now there's going to be a pankee,*
> *Now we're going to fry a pankye."*

Then she took three eggs and threw them up in the air. One fell down on her head and broke so that the yolk ran into her eyes, but the others she caught skillfully in a bowl, where they smashed to pieces.

"I always did hear that egg yolk was good for the hair," said Pippi, wiping her eyes. "You wait and see—mine will soon begin to grow so fast it crackles. As a matter of fact, in Brazil all the people go about with eggs in their hair. And there are no bald-headed people. Only once was there a man who was so foolish that he ate his eggs instead of rubbing them on his hair. He became completely bald-headed, and when he showed himself on the street there was such a riot that the radio police were called out."

While she was speaking Pippi had neatly picked the eggshells out of the bowl with her fingers. Now she took a bath brush that hung on the wall and began to beat the pancake batter so hard that it splashed all over the walls. At last she poured what was left onto a griddle that stood on the stove.

When the pancake was brown on one side she tossed it halfway up to the ceiling, so that it turned

right around in the air, and then she caught it on the griddle again. And when it was ready she threw it straight across the kitchen right onto a plate that stood on the table.

"Eat!" she cried. "Eat before it gets cold!"

And Tommy and Annika ate and thought it a very good pancake.

Afterward Pippi invited them to step into the parlor. There was only one piece of furniture in there. It was a huge chest with many tiny drawers. Pippi opened the drawers and showed Tommy and Annika all the treasures she kept there. There were wonderful birds' eggs, strange shells and stones, pretty little boxes, lovely silver mirrors, pearl necklaces, and many other things that Pippi and her father had bought on their journeys around the world. Pippi gave each of her new playmates a little gift to remember her by. Tommy got a dagger with a shimmering mother-of-pearl handle, and Annika a little box with a cover decorated with pink shells. In the box there was a ring with a green stone.

"Suppose you go home now," said Pippi, "so that you can come back tomorrow. Because if you don't go home you can't come back, and that would be a shame."

Tommy and Annika agreed that it would indeed. So they went home—past the horse, who had now eaten up all the oats, and out through the gate of Villa Villekulla. Mr. Nilsson waved his hat at them as they left.

2.
Pippi Is a Thing-finder and Gets into a Fight

ANNIKA woke up early the next morning. She jumped out of bed and ran over to Tommy.

"Wake up, Tommy," she cried, pulling him by the arm, "wake up and let's go and see that funny girl with the big shoes."

Tommy was wide awake in an instant.

"I knew, even while I was sleeping, that something exciting was going to happen today, but I didn't remember what it was," he said as he yanked off his pajama jacket. Off they went to the bathroom; washed themselves and brushed their teeth much faster than usual; had their clothes on in a twinkling; and a whole hour before their mother expected them came sliding down the bannister and

26

landed at the breakfast table. Down they sat and announced that they wanted their hot chocolate right off that very moment.

"What's going to happen today that you're in such a hurry?" asked their mother.

"We're going to see the new girl next door," said Tommy.

"We may stay all day," said Annika.

That morning Pippi was busy making *peppar-kakor*—that's a kind of Swedish cooky. She had made an enormous amount of dough and rolled it out on the kitchen floor.

"Because," said Pippi to her little monkey, "what earthly use is a baking board when one plans to make at least five hundred cookies?"

And there she lay on the floor, cutting out cooky hearts for dear life.

"Stop climbing around in the dough, Mr. Nilsson," she said crossly just as the doorbell rang.

Pippi ran and opened the door. She was white as a miller from top to toe, and when she shook hands heartily with Tommy and Annika a whole cloud of flour blew over them.

"So nice you called," she said and shook her apron—so there came another cloud of flour.

Tommy and Annika got so much in their throats that they could not help coughing.

"What are you doing?" asked Tommy.

"Well, if I say that I'm sweeping the chimney, you won't believe me, you're so clever," said Pippi. "Fact is, I'm baking. But I'll soon be done. You can sit on the woodbox for a while."

Pippi could work fast, she could. Tommy and Annika sat and watched how she went through the dough, how she threw the cookies onto the cooky pans, and swung the pans into the oven. They thought it was good as a circus.

"Done!" said Pippi at last and shut the oven door on the last pans with a bang.

"What are we going to do now?" asked Tommy.

"I don't know what you are going to do," said Pippi, "but I know I can't lie around and be lazy. I am a Thing-finder, and when you're a Thing-finder you don't have a minute to spare."

"What did you say you are?" asked Annika.

"A Thing-finder."

"What's that?" asked Tommy.

"Somebody who hunts for things, naturally. What else could it be?" said Pippi as she swept all the flour left on the floor into a little pile.

"The whole world is full of things, and somebody has to look for them. And that's just what a Thing-finder does," she finished.

"What kind of things?" asked Annika.

"Oh, all kinds," said Pippi. "Lumps of gold, ostrich feathers, dead rats, candy snapcrackers, and little tiny screws, and things like that."

Tommy and Annika thought it sounded as if it would be fun and wanted very much to be Thing-finders too, although Tommy did say he hoped he'd find a lump of gold and not a little tiny screw.

"We shall see what we shall see," said Pippi. "One always finds something. But we've got to hurry up and get going so that other Thing-finders don't pick up all the lumps of gold around here before we get them."

All three Thing-finders now set out. They decided that it would be best to begin hunting around the houses in the neighborhood, because Pippi said that although it could perfectly well happen that one might find a little screw deep in the woods, still the very best things were usually found where people were living.

"Though, for that matter," she said, "I've seen it the other way around too. I remember once when

I was out hunting for things in the jungles of Borneo. Right in the heart of the forest, where no human being had ever before set foot, what do you suppose I found? Why, a very fine wooden leg! I gave it away later to a one-legged old man, and he said that a wooden leg like that wasn't to be had for love nor money."

Tommy and Annika looked at Pippi to see just how a Thing-finder acted. Pippi ran from one side of the road to the other, shaded her eyes with her hand, and hunted and hunted. Sometimes she crawled about on her hands and knees, stuck her hands in between the pickets of a fence, and then said in a disappointed tone, "Oh, dear! I was sure I saw a lump of gold."

"May we really take everything we find?" asked Annika.

"Yes, everything that is lying on the ground," said Pippi.

Presently they came to an old man lying asleep on the lawn outside his cottage.

"There," said Pippi, "that man is lying on the ground and we have found him. We'll take him!"

Tommy and Annika were utterly terrified.

"No, no, Pippi, we can't take an old gentleman.

We couldn't possibly," said Tommy. "Anyway, whatever would we do with him?"

"What would we do with him? Oh, there are plenty of things we could do with him. We could keep him in a little rabbit hutch instead of a rabbit and feed him on dandelions. But if you don't want to, I don't care. Though it does bother me to think that some other Thing-finder may come along and grab him."

They went on. Suddenly Pippi gave a terrific yell. "Well, I never saw the like," she cried and picked up from the grass a rusty old tin can. "What a find! What a find! Cans—that's something you can never have too many of."

Tommy looked at the can doubtfully. "What can you use it for?"

"Oh, you can use it in all sorts of ways," said Pippi. "One way is to put cookies in it. Then it becomes a delightful Jar with Cookies. Another way is not to put cookies in it. Then it becomes a Jar without Cookies. That certainly isn't quite so delightful, but still that's good too."

She examined the can, which was indeed rusty and had a hole in the bottom.

"It looks almost as if this were a Jar without

Cookies," she said thoughtfully. "But you can put it over your head and pretend that it is midnight."

And that is just what she did. With the can on her head she wandered around the block like a little metal tower and never stopped until she stumbled over a low wire fence and fell flat on her stomach. There was a big crash when the tin can hit the ground.

"Now, see that!" said Pippi and took off the can. "If I hadn't had this thing on me, I'd have fallen flat on my face and hurt myself terribly."

"Yes," said Annika, "but if you had not had the can on your head, then you wouldn't have tripped on the wire fence in the first place."

Before she had finished speaking there was another triumphant cry from Pippi, who was holding up an empty spool of thread.

"This seems to be my lucky day," she said. "Such a sweet, sweet little spool to blow soap bubbles with or to hang around my neck for a necklace. I'll go home and make one this very minute."

However, just at that moment the gate of one of the cottages nearby opened and a boy came rushing out. He looked scared, and that was no wonder, because head over heels after him came five other boys. They soon caught him and pushed him against the fence, and all five began to punch and hit him. He cried and held his arms in front of his face to protect himself.

"Give it to him! Give it to him!" cried the oldest and strongest of the boys, "so that he will never dare to show himself on this street again."

"Oh," said Annika, "it's Willie they're hurting. Oh, how can they be so mean?"

"It's that awful Bengt. He's always in a fight," said Tommy. "And five against one—what cowards!"

Pippi went up to the boys and tapped Bengt on the back with her forefinger. "Hello, there," she said. "What's the idea? Are you trying to make hash out of little Willie with all five of you jumping on him at once?"

Bengt turned around and saw a little girl he had never seen before: a wild-looking little stranger who dared to touch him. For a while he stood and gaped at her in astonishment; then a broad grin spread over his face. "Boys," he said, "boys, let Willie alone and take a look at this girl. What a babe!"

He slapped his knees and laughed, and in an instant they had all flocked around Pippi, all except

Willie, who wiped away his tears and walked cautiously over to stand beside Tommy.

"Have you ever seen hair like hers? Red as fire! And such shoes," Bengt continued. "Can't I borrow one? I'd like to go out rowing and I haven't any boat." He took hold of one of Pippi's braids but dropped it instantly and cried, "Ouch, I burned myself."

Then all five boys joined hands around Pippi, jumping up and down and screaming, "Redhead! Redhead!"

Pippi stood in the middle of the ring and smiled in the friendliest way. Bengt had hoped she would get mad and begin to cry. At least she ought to have looked scared. When nothing happened he gave her a push.

"I don't think you have a very nice way with ladies," said Pippi. And she lifted him in her strong arms—high in the air—and carried him to a birch tree and hung him over a branch. Then she took the next boy and hung him over another branch. The next one she set on a gatepost outside a cottage, and the next she threw right over a fence so that he landed in a flower bed. The last of the fighters she put in a tiny toy cart that stood by the road. Then

Pippi, Tommy, Annika, and Willie stood and looked at the boys for a while. The boys were absolutely speechless with fright.

And Pippi said, "You are cowards. Five of you attack one boy. That's cowardly. Then you begin to push a helpless little girl around. Oh, how mean!

"Come now, we'll go home," she said to Tommy and Annika. And to Willie, "If they try to hurt you again, you come and tell me." And to Bengt, who sat up in the tree and didn't dare to stir, she said, "Is there anything else you have to say about my hair or my shoes? If so, you'd better say it now before I go home."

But Bengt had nothing more to say about Pippi's shoes, or about her hair either. So Pippi took her can in one hand and her spool in the other and went away, followed by Tommy and Annika.

When they were back home in Pippi's garden Pippi said, "Dear me, how awful! Here I found two beautiful things and you didn't get anything. You must hunt a little more. Tommy, why don't you look in that old hollow tree? Old trees are usually about the best places of all for Thing-finders."

Tommy said that he didn't believe he and Annika would ever find anything, but to please Pippi he put his hand slowly down into the hollow tree trunk.

"Goodness!" he cried, utterly amazed, and pulled out his hand. In it he held a little notebook with a leather cover. In a special loop there was a little silver pencil.

"Well, that's queer," said Tommy.

"Now, see that!" said Pippi. "There's nothing so nice as being a Thing-finder. It's a wonder there aren't more people that take it up. They'll be tailors and shoemakers and chimney sweeps, and such like—but Thing-finders, no indeed, that isn't good enough for them!"

And then she said to Annika, "Why don't you feel in that old tree stump? One practically always finds things in old tree stumps."

Annika stuck her hand down in the stump and almost immediately got hold of a red coral necklace. She and Tommy stood open-mouthed for a long time, they were so astonished. They thought that hereafter they would be Thing-finders every single day.

Pippi had been up half the night before, playing ball, and now she suddenly felt sleepy. "I think I'll have to go and take a nap," she said. "Can't you come with me and tuck me in?"

When Pippi was sitting on the edge of the bed, taking off her shoes, she looked at them thoughtfully and said, "He was going out rowing, he said, that old Bengt." She snorted disdainfully. "I'll teach him to row, indeed I will. Another time."

"Say, Pippi," said Tommy respectfully, "why do you wear such big shoes?"

"So I can wiggle my toes, of course," she answered.

Then she crept into bed. She always slept with her feet on the pillow and her head way down under the quilt. "That's the way they sleep in Guatemala," she announced. "And it's the only real way to sleep. See, like this, I can wiggle my toes when I'm sleeping too.

"Can you go to sleep without a lullaby?" she went on. "I always have to sing to myself for a while; otherwise I can't sleep a wink."

Tommy and Annika heard a humming sound under the quilt; it was Pippi singing herself to sleep. Quietly and cautiously they tiptoed out so that they would not disturb her. In the doorway they turned to take a last look toward the bed. They could see nothing of Pippi except her feet resting on the pillow. There she lay, wiggling her toes emphatically.

Tommy and Annika ran home. Annika held her coral necklace tightly in her hand.

"That certainly was queer," she said. "Tommy, you don't suppose—*do* you suppose that Pippi had put these things in place beforehand?"

"You never can tell," said Tommy. "You just never can tell about anything when it comes to Pippi."

3.
Pippi
Plays Tag
with
Some Policemen

I<small>T</small> soon became known throughout the little town that a nine-year-old girl was living all by herself in Villa Villekulla, and all the ladies and gentlemen in the town thought this would never do. All children must have someone to advise them, and all children must go to school to learn the multiplication tables. So the ladies and gentlemen decided that the little girl in Villa Villekulla must immediately be placed in a children's home.

One lovely afternoon Pippi had invited Tommy and Annika over for afternoon coffee and *pepparkakor*. She had spread the party out on the front steps. It was so sunny and beautiful there, and the

air was filled with the fragrance of the flowers in
Pippi's garden. Mr. Nilsson climbed around on the
porch railing, and every now and then the horse
stuck out his head so that he'd be invited to have a
cooky.

"Oh, isn't it glorious to be alive?" said Pippi,
stretching out her legs as far as she could reach.

Just at that moment two police officers in full uniform came in through the gate.

"Hurray," said Pippi, "this must be my lucky
day too! Policemen are the very best things I know.
Next to rhubarb pudding." And with her face beam-
ing she went to meet them.

"Is this the girl who has moved into Villa Villekulla?" asked one of the policemen.

"Quite the contrary," said Pippi. "This is a tiny
little auntie who lives on the third floor at the other
end of the town."

She said that only because she wanted to have a
little fun with the policemen, but they didn't think
it was funny at all.

They said she shouldn't be such a smarty. And then
they went on to tell her that some nice people in the
town were arranging for her to get into a children's
home.

"I already have a place in a children's home," said Pippi.

"What?" asked one of the policemen. "Has it been arranged already then? What children's home?"

"This one," said Pippi haughtily. "I am a child and this is my home; therefore it is a children's home, and I have room enough here, plenty of room."

"Dear child," said the policeman, smiling, "you don't understand. You must get into a real children's home and have someone look after you."

"Is one allowed to bring horses to your children's home?" asked Pippi.

"No, of course not," said the policeman.

"That's what I thought," said Pippi sadly. "Well, what about monkeys?"

"Of course not. You ought to realize that."

"Well then," said Pippi, "you'll have to get kids for your children's home somewhere else. I certainly don't intend to move there."

"But don't you understand that you must go to school?"

"Why?"

"To learn things, of course."

"What sort of things?" asked Pippi.

"All sorts," said the policeman. "Lots of useful

things—the multiplication tables, for instance."

"I have got along fine without any pluttifikation tables for nine years," said Pippi, "and I guess I'll get along without it from now on, too."

"Yes, but just think how embarrassing it will be for you to be so ignorant. Imagine when you grow up and somebody asks you what the capital of Portugal is, and you can't answer!"

"Oh, I can answer all right," said Pippi. "I'll answer like this: 'If you are so bound and determined to find out what the capital of Portugal is, then, for goodness' sakes, write directly to Portugal and ask.'"

"Yes, but don't you think that you would be sorry not to know it yourself?"

"Oh, probably," said Pippi. "No doubt I should lie awake nights and wonder and wonder, 'What in the world is the capital of Portugal?' But one can't be having fun all the time," she continued, bending over and standing on her hands for a change. "For that matter, I've been in Lisbon with my papa," she added, still standing upside down, for she could talk that way too.

But then one of the policemen said that Pippi certainly didn't need to think she could do just as she pleased. She must come to the children's home, and immediately. He went up to her and took hold of her arm, but Pippi freed herself quickly, touched him lightly, and said, "Tag!" Before he could wink an eye she had climbed up on the porch railing and from there onto the balcony above the porch. The policemen couldn't quite see themselves getting up the same way, and so they rushed into the house and up the stairs, but by the time they had reached the balcony Pippi was halfway up the roof. She climbed up the shingles almost as if she were a little monkey herself. In a moment she was up on the ridgepole and from there jumped easily to the chimney. Down on the balcony stood the two policemen, scratching their heads, and on the lawn stood Tommy and Annika, staring at Pippi.

"Isn't it fun to play tag?" cried Pippi. "And weren't you nice to come over. It certainly *is* my lucky day today too."

When the policemen had stood there a while wondering what to do, they went and got a ladder, leaned it against one of the gables of the house and then climbed up, first one policeman and then the other, to get Pippi down. They looked a little scared when they climbed out on the ridgepole and, carefully balancing themselves, went step by step, toward Pippi.

"Don't be scared," cried Pippi. "There's nothing to be afraid of. It's just fun."

When the policemen were a few steps away from Pippi, down she jumped from the chimney and, screeching and laughing, ran along the ridgepole to the opposite gable. A few feet from the house stood a tree.

"Now I'm going to dive," she cried and jumped right down into the green crown of the tree, caught fast hold of a branch, swung back and forth a while, and then let herself fall to the ground. Quick as a wink she dashed around to the other side of the house and took away the ladder.

The policemen had looked a little foolish when Pippi jumped, but they looked even more so when they had balanced themselves backward along the ridgepole and were about to climb down the ladder. At first they were very angry at Pippi, who stood on the ground looking up at them, and they told her in no uncertain terms to get the ladder and be quick about it, or she would soon get something she wasn't looking for.

"Why are you so cross at me?" asked Pippi

reproachfully. "We're just playing tag, aren't we?"

The policemen thought a while, and at last one of them said, "Oh, come on, won't you be a good girl and put the ladder back so that we can get down?"

"Of course I will," said Pippi and put the ladder back instantly. "And when you get down we can all drink coffee and have a happy time."

But the policemen were certainly tricky, because the minute they were down on the ground again they pounced on Pippi and cried, "Now you'll get it, you little brat!"

"Oh, no, I'm sorry. I haven't time to play any longer," said Pippi. "But it was fun."

Then she took hold of the policemen by their belts and carried them down the garden path, out through the gate, and onto the street. There she set them down, and it was quite some time before they were ready to get up again.

"Wait a minute," she cried and ran into the kitchen and came back with two cooky hearts. "Would you like a taste?" she asked. "It doesn't matter that they are a little burned, does it?"

Then she went back to Tommy and Annika, who stood there wide-eyed and just couldn't get over what they had seen. And the policemen hurried back

to the town and told all the ladies and gentlemen that Pippi wasn't quite fit for an orphanage. (They didn't tell that they had been up on the roof.) And the ladies and gentlemen decided that it would be best after all to let Pippi remain in Villa Villekulla, and if she wanted to go to school she could make the arrangements herself.

But Pippi and Tommy and Annika had a very pleasant afternoon. They went back to their interrupted coffee party. Pippi stuffed herself with fourteen cookies and then she said, "They weren't what I mean by real policemen. No sirree! Altogether too much talk about children's homes and pluttifikation and Lisbon."

Afterward she lifted the horse down on the ground and they rode on him, all three. At first Annika was afraid and didn't want to, but when she saw what fun Tommy and Pippi were having, she let Pippi lift her up on the horse's back. The horse trotted round and round in the garden, and Tommy sang, "Here come the Swedes with a clang and a bang."

When Tommy and Annika had gone to bed that night Tommy said, "Annika, don't you think it's good that Pippi moved here?"

"Oh, *yes*," said Annika.

"I don't even remember what we used to play before she came, do you?"

"Oh, sure, we played croquet and things like that," said Annika. "But it's lots more fun with Pippi around, I think. And with horses and things."

4.
Pippi Goes to School

O F course Tommy and Annika went to school. Each morning at eight o'clock they trotted off, hand in hand, swinging their schoolbags.

At that time Pippi was usually grooming her horse or dressing Mr. Nilsson in his little suit. Or else she was taking her morning exercises, which meant turning forty-three somersaults in a row. Then she would sit down on the kitchen table and, utterly happy, drink a large cup of coffee and eat a piece of bread and cheese.

Tommy and Annika always looked longingly toward Villa Villekulla as they started off to school. They would much rather have gone to play with

Pippi. If only Pippi had been going to school too; that would have been something else again.

"Just think what fun we could have on the way home from school," said Tommy.

"Yes, and on the way to school too," said Annika.

The more they thought about it the worse they felt to think that Pippi did not go to school, and at last they determined to try to persuade her to begin.

"You can't imagine what a nice teacher we have," said Tommy artfully to Pippi one afternoon when he and Annika had come for a visit at Villa Villekulla after they had finished their homework.

"If you only knew what fun it is in school!" Annika added. "I'd die if I couldn't go to school."

Pippi sat on a hassock, bathing her feet in a tub. She said nothing but just wiggled her toes for a while so that the water splashed around everywhere.

"You don't have to stay so very long," continued Tommy; "just until two o'clock."

"Yes, and besides, we get Christmas vacation and Easter vacation and summer vacation," said Annika.

Pippi bit her big toe thoughtfully but still said nothing. Suddenly, as if she had made some decision, she poured all the water out on the kitchen floor, so that Mr. Nilsson, who sat near her playing with a mirror, got his pants absolutely soaked.

"It's not fair!" said Pippi sternly without paying any attention to Mr. Nilsson's puzzled air about his wet pants. "It is absolutely unfair! I don't intend to stand it!"

"What's the matter now?" asked Tommy.

"In four months it will be Christmas, and then you'll have Christmas vacation. But I, what'll I get?" Pippi's voice sounded sad. "No Christmas vacation, not even the tiniest bit of a Christmas vacation," she complained. "Something will have to be done about that. Tomorrow morning I'll begin school."

Tommy and Annika clapped their hands with delight. "Hurrah! We'll wait for you outside our gate at eight o'clock."

"Oh, no," said Pippi, "I can't begin as early as that. And besides, I'm going to ride to school."

And ride she did. Exactly at ten o'clock the next day she lifted her horse off the porch, and a little later all the people in the town ran to their windows to see what horse it was that was running away. That is to say, they thought he was running away, but it was only Pippi in a bit of a hurry to get to school.

She galloped wildly into the schoolyard, jumped off the horse, tied him to a tree, and burst into the schoolroom with such a noise and a clatter that Tommy and Annika and all their classmates jumped in their seats.

"Hi, there," cried Pippi, waving her big hat. "Did I get here in time for pluttifikation?"

Tommy and Annika had told their teacher that a new girl named Pippi Longstocking was coming; and the teacher had already heard about Pippi in the little town. As she was a very pleasant teacher, she had decided to do all she could to make Pippi happy in school.

Pippi threw herself down on a vacant bench without having been invited to do so, but the teacher paid no attention to her heedless way. She simply said in a very friendly voice, "Welcome to school, little Pippi. I hope that you will enjoy yourself here and learn a great deal."

"Yes, and I hope I'll get some Christmas vacation," said Pippi. "That is the reason I've come. It's only fair, you know."

"If you would first tell me your whole name," said the teacher, "then I'll register you in school."

"My name is Pippilotta Delicatessa Window-shade Mackrelmint Efraim's Daughter Long-stocking, daughter of Captain Efraim Longstocking, formerly the Terror of the Sea, now a cannibal king. Pippi is really only a nickname, because Papa thought that Pippilotta was too long to say."

"Indeed?" said the teacher. "Well, then we shall call you Pippi too. But now," she continued, "suppose we test you a little and see what you know. You are a big girl and no doubt know a great deal already. Let us begin with arithmetic. Pippi, can you tell me what seven and five are?"

Pippi, astonished and dismayed, looked at her and said, "Well, if you don't know that yourself, you needn't think I'm going to tell you."

All the children stared in horror at Pippi, and the teacher explained that one couldn't answer that way in school.

"I beg your pardon," said Pippi contritely. "I didn't know that. I won't do it again."

"No, let us hope not," said the teacher. "And now I will tell you that seven and five are twelve."

"See that!" said Pippi. "You knew it yourself. Why are you asking then?"

The teacher decided to act as if nothing unusual

were happening and went on with her examination.

"Well now, Pippi, how much do you think eight and four are?"

"Oh, about sixty-seven," hazarded Pippi.

"Of course not," said the teacher. "Eight and four are twelve."

"Well now, really, my dear little woman," said Pippi, "that is carrying things too far. You just said that seven and five are twelve. There should be some rhyme and reason to things even in school. Furthermore, if you are so childishly interested in that foolishness, why don't you sit down in a corner by yourself and do arithmetic and leave us alone so we can play tag?"

The teacher decided there was no point in trying to teach Pippi any more arithmetic. She began to ask the other children the arithmetic questions.

"Can Tommy answer this one?" she asked. "If Lisa has seven apples and Axel has nine apples, how many apples do they have together?"

"Yes, you tell, Tommy," Pippi interrupted, "and tell me too, if Lisa gets a stomach-ache and Axel gets more stomach-ache, whose fault is it and where did they get hold of the apples in the first place?"

The teacher tried to pretend that she hadn't heard

and turned to Annika. "Now, Annika, here's an example for you: Gustav was with his schoolmates on a picnic. He had a quarter when he started out and seven cents when he got home. How much did he spend?"

"Yes, indeed," said Pippi, "and I also want to know why he was so extravagant, and if it was pop he bought, and if he washed his ears properly before he left home."

The teacher decided to give up arithmetic altogether. She thought maybe Pippi would prefer to learn to read. So she took out a pretty little card with a picture of an ibex on it. In front of the ibex's nose was the letter "i."

"Now, Pippi," she said briskly, "you'll see something jolly. You see here an ibex. And the letter in front of this ibex is called 'i.' "

"That I'll never believe," said Pippi. "I think it looks exactly like a straight line with a little fly speck over it. But what I'd really like to know is, what has the ibex to do with the fly speck?"

The teacher took out another card with a picture of a snake on it and told Pippi that the letter on that was an "s."

"Speaking of snakes," said Pippi, "I'll never, ever

forget the time I had a fight with a huge snake in India. You can't imagine what a dreadful snake it was, fourteen yards long and mad as a hornet, and every day he ate up five Indians and then two little children for dessert, and one time he came and wanted me for dessert, and he wound himself around me—uhhh!—but I've been around a bit, I said, and hit him in the head, bang, and then he hissed uiuiuiuiuiuiuiuitch, and then I hit him again, and bingo! he was dead, and, indeed, so that is the letter 's'—most remarkable!"

Pippi had to stop to get her breath. And the teacher, who had now begun to think that Pippi was an unruly and troublesome child, decided that the class should have drawing for a while. Surely Pippi could sit still and be quiet and draw, thought the teacher. She took out paper and pencils and passed them out to the children.

"Now you may draw whatever you wish," she said and sat down at her desk and began to correct copybooks. In a little while she looked up to see how the drawing was going. All the children sat looking at Pippi, who lay flat on the floor, drawing to her heart's content.

"But, Pippi," said the teacher impatiently, "why

in the world aren't you drawing on your paper?"

"I filled that long ago. There isn't room enough for my whole horse on that little snip of a paper," said Pippi. "Just now I'm working on his front legs, but when I get to his tail I guess I'll have to go out in the hall."

The teacher thought hard for a while. "Suppose instead we all sing a little song," she suggested.

All the children stood up by their seats except Pippi; she stayed where she was on the floor. "You go ahead and sing," she said. "I'll rest myself a while. Too much learning breaks even the healthiest."

But now the teacher's patience came to an end. She told all the children to go out into the yard so she could talk to Pippi alone.

When the teacher and Pippi were alone, Pippi got up and walked to the desk. "Do you know what?" she said. "It was awfully jolly to come to school to find out what it was like. But I don't think I care about going to school any more, Christmas vacation or no Christmas vacation. There's altogether too many apples and ibexes and snakes and things like that. It makes me dizzy in the head. I hope that you, Teacher, won't be sorry."

But the teacher said she certainly was sorry, most of all because Pippi wouldn't behave decently; and that any girl who acted as badly as Pippi did wouldn't be allowed to go to school even if she wanted to ever so.

"Have I behaved badly?" asked Pippi, much astonished. "Goodness, I didn't know that," she added and looked very sad. And nobody could look as sad as Pippi when she was sad. She stood silent for a while, and then she said in a trembling voice, "You understand, Teacher, don't you, that when you have a mother who's an angel and a father who is a cannibal king, and when you have sailed on the ocean all your whole life, then you don't know just how to behave in school with all the apples and ibexes."

Then the teacher said she understood and didn't feel annoyed with Pippi any longer, and maybe Pippi could come back to school when she was a little older. Pippi positively beamed with delight. "I think you are awfully nice, Teacher. And here is something for you."

Out of her pocket Pippi took a lovely little gold watch and laid it on the desk. The teacher said she couldn't possibly accept such a valuable gift from Pippi, but Pippi replied, "You've got to take it;

otherwise I'll come back again tomorrow, and that would be a pretty how-do-you-do."

Then Pippi rushed out to the schoolyard and jumped on her horse. All the children gathered around to pat the horse and see her off.

"You ought to know about the schools in Argentina," said Pippi, looking down at the children. "That's where you should go. Easter vacation begins three days after Christmas vacation ends, and when Easter vacation is over there are three days and then it's summer vacation. Summer vacation ends on the first of November, and then you have a tough time until Christmas vacation begins on November 11. But you can stand that because there are at least no lessons. It is strictly against the law to have lessons in Argentina. Once in a while it happens that some Argentine kid sneaks into a closet and sits there studying a lesson, but it's just too bad for him if his mother finds him. Arithmetic they don't have at all in the schools, and if there is any kid who knows what seven and five are he has to stand in the corner all day—that is, if he's foolish enough to let the teacher know that he knows. Reading they have only on Friday, and even then only if they have some books, which they never have."

"But what do they do in school?" asked one little boy.

"Eat caramels," said Pippi decidedly. "There is a long pipe that goes from a caramel factory nearby directly into the schoolroom, and caramels keep shooting out of it all day long so the children have all they can do to eat them up."

"Yes, but what does the teacher do?" asked one little girl.

"Takes the paper off the caramels for the children, of course," said Pippi. "You didn't suppose they did it themselves, did you? Hardly. They don't even go to school themselves; they send their brothers." Pippi waved her big hat.

"So long, kids," she cried gaily. "Now you won't see me for a while. But always remember how many apples Axel had or you'll be sorry."

With a ringing laugh Pippi rode out through the gate so wildly that the pebbles whirled around the horse's hoofs and the windowpanes rattled in the schoolhouse.

5.
Pippi Sits on the Gate and Climbs a Tree

OUTSIDE Villa Villekulla sat Pippi, Tommy, and Annika. Pippi sat on one gatepost, Annika on the other, and Tommy sat on the gate. It was a warm and beautiful day toward the end of August. A pear tree that grew close to the fence stretched its branches so low down that the children could sit and pick the best little red-gold pears without any trouble at all. They munched and ate and spit pear cores out onto the road.

Villa Villekulla stood just at the edge of the little town, where the street turned into a country road. The people in the little town loved to go walking out Villa Villekulla way, for the country out there was so beautiful.

As the children were sitting there eating pears, a girl came walking along the road from town. When she saw the children she stopped and asked, "Have you seen my papa go by?"

"M-m-m," said Pippi. "How did he look? Did he have blue eyes?"

"Yes," said the girl.

"Medium large, not too tall and not too short?"

"Yes," said the girl.

"Black hat and black shoes?"

"Yes, exactly," said the girl eagerly.

"No, that one we haven't seen," said Pippi decidedly.

The girl looked crestfallen and went off without a word.

"Wait a minute," shrieked Pippi after her. "Was he bald-headed?"

"No, he certainly was not," said the girl crossly.

"Lucky for him!" said Pippi and spit out a pear core.

The girl hurried away, but then Pippi shouted, "Did he have big ears that reached way down to his shoulders?"

"No," said the girl and turned and came running back in amazement. "You don't mean to say that you have seen a man walk by with such big ears?"

"I have never seen anyone who walks with his ears," said Pippi. "All the people I know walk with their feet."

"Oh, don't be silly! I mean have you really seen a man who has such big ears?"

"No," said Pippi, "there isn't anybody with such big ears. It would be ridiculous. How would they look? It isn't possible to have such big ears. At least not in this country," she added after a thoughtful pause. "Of course in China it's a little different. I once saw a Chinese in Shanghai. His ears were so big that he could use them for a cape. When it rained he just crawled in under his ears and was as warm and snug as you please. Of course his ears didn't have it so good. If it was very bad weather he used to invite his friends to camp under his ears. There they sat and sang sad songs while the rain poured down. They liked him a lot because of his ears. His name was Hai Shang. You should have seen Hai Shang run to work in the morning. He always came dashing in at the last minute because he loved to sleep late, and you can't imagine how funny he looked, rushing in with his ears flying behind him like two big golden sails."

The girl had stopped and stood open-mouthed listening to Pippi. And Tommy and Annika forgot to eat any more pears, they were so utterly absorbed in the story.

"He had more children than he could count, and the littlest one was named Peter," said Pippi.

"Oh, but a Chinese baby can't be called Peter," interrupted Tommy.

"That's just what his wife said to him, 'A Chinese baby can't be called Peter.' But Hai Shang was dreadfully stubborn, and he said that the baby should be called Peter or Nothing. And then he sat down in a corner and pulled his ears over his head and howled. And his poor wife had to give in, of course, and the kid was called Peter."

"Really?" said Annika.

"It was the hatefulest kid in all Shanghai," continued Pippi. "Fussy about his food, so that his mother was most unhappy. You know, of course, that they eat swallows' nests in China? And there sat his mother, with a whole plate full of swallows' nests, trying to feed him. 'Now, little Peter,' she said, 'come, we'll eat a swallows' nest for Daddy.' But Peter just shut his mouth tight and shook his head. At last Hai Shang was so angry that he said that no new food should be prepared for Peter until he had eaten a swallows' nest for Daddy. And when Hai Shang said something, that was that. The same swallows' nest rode in and out of the kitchen from May until October. On the fourteenth of July his mother begged to be allowed to give Peter a couple of meatballs, but Hai Shang said no."

"Nonsense!" said the girl in the road.

"Yes, that's just what Hai Shang said," continued Pippi. " 'Nonsense,' he said, 'it's perfectly plain that the child can eat the swallows' nest if he'll only stop being so stubborn.' But Peter kept his mouth shut tight from May to October."

"But how could he live?" asked Tommy, astonished.

"He couldn't live," said Pippi. "He died. Of Plain Common Ordinary Pigheadedness. The eighteenth of October. And was buried the nineteenth. And on the twentieth a swallow flew in through the window and laid an egg in the nest, which was standing on the table. So it came in handy after all. No harm done," said Pippi happily. Then she looked thoughtfully at the bewildered girl, who still stood in the road.

"Why do you look so funny?" asked Pippi.

"What's the matter? You don't really think that I'm sitting here telling lies, do you? What? Just tell me if you do," said Pippi threateningly and rolled up her sleeves.

"Oh, no, indeed," said the girl, terrified. "I don't really mean that you are lying, but—"

"No?" said Pippi. "But it's just what I'm doing. I'm lying so my tongue is turning black. Do you really think that a child can live without food from May to October? To be sure, I know they can get along without food for three or four months all right. But from May to October! It's just foolish to think that. You must know that's a lie. You mustn't let people fool you like that."

Then the girl left without turning around again.

"People will believe anything," said Pippi to Tommy and Annika. "From May until October! That's ridiculous!"

Then she called after the girl, "No, we haven't seen your papa. We haven't seen a single bald-headed person all day. But yesterday seventeen of them went by. Arm in arm."

Pippi's garden was really lovely. You couldn't say it was well kept, but there were wonderful grass plots that were never cut, and old rosebushes that

,ere full of white and yellow and pink roses—perhaps not such fine roses, but oh, how sweet they smelled! A good many fruit trees grew there too, and, best of all, several ancient oaks and elms that were excellent for climbing.

The trees in Tommy's and Annika's garden were not very good for climbing, and besides, their mother was always so afraid they would fall and get hurt that they had never climbed much. But now Pippi said, "Suppose we climb up in the big oak tree?"

Tommy jumped down from the gate at once, delighted with the suggestion. Annika was a little hesitant, but when she saw that the trunk had nubbly places to climb on, she too thought it would be fun to try.

A few feet above the ground the oak divided into two branches, and right there was a place just like a little room. Before long all three children were sitting there. Over their heads the oak spread out its crown like a great green roof.

"We could drink coffee here," said Pippi. "I'll skip in and make a little."

Tommy and Annika clapped their hands and shouted, "Bravo!"

In a little while Pippi had the coffee ready. She

had made buns the day before. She came and stood under the oak and began to toss up coffee cups. Tommy and Annika caught them. Only sometimes it was the oak that caught them, and so two cups were broken. Pippi ran in to get new ones. Next it was the buns' turn, and for a while the air was full of flying buns. At least they didn't break. At last Pippi climbed up with the coffee pot in one hand. She had cream in a little bottle in her pocket, and sugar in a little box.

Tommy and Annika thought coffee had never tasted so good before. They were not allowed to drink it every day—only when they were at a party. And now they were at a party. Annika spilled a little coffee in her lap. First it was warm and wet, and then it was cold and wet, but that didn't matter to her.

When they had finished, Pippi threw the cups down on the grass. "I want to see how strong the china they make these days is," she said. Strangely enough, one cup and three saucers held together, and only the spout of the coffee pot broke off.

Presently Pippi decided to climb a little higher.

"Can you beat this?" she cried suddenly. "The tree is hollow."

There in the trunk was a big hole, which the leaves had hidden from the children's sight.

"Oh, may I climb up and look too?" called Tommy. But there was no answer.

"Pippi, where are you?" he cried, worried.

Then they heard Pippi's voice, not from above but from way down below. It sounded as if it came from under the ground.

"I'm inside the tree. It is hollow clear down to the ground. If I peek out through a little crack I can see the coffee pot outside on the grass."

"Oh, how will you get up again?" cried Annika.

"I'm never coming up," said Pippi. "I'm going to stay here until I retire and get a pension. And you'll have to throw my food down through that hole up there. Five or six times a day."

Annika began to cry.

"Why be sorry? Why complain?" said Pippi. "You come down here too, and then we can play that we are pining away in a dungeon."

"Never in this world!" said Annika, and to be on the safe side she climbed right down out of the tree.

"Annika, I can see you through the crack," cried Pippi. "Don't step on the coffee pot; it's an old well-mannered coffee pot that never did anyone any harm. It can't help that it doesn't have a spout any longer."

Annika went up to the tree trunk, and through a little crack she saw the very tip of Pippi's finger. This comforted her a good deal, but she was still worried.

"Pippi, can't you really get up?' she asked.

Pippi's finger disappeared, and in less than a minute her face popped out of the hole up in the tree.

"Maybe I can if I try very hard," she said and parted the foliage with her hands.

˙ "If it's as easy as all that to get up," said Tommy, who was still up in the tree, "then I want to come down and pine away a little too."

"Wait," said Pippi, "I think we'll get a ladder."

She crawled out of the hole and hurried down the tree. Then she ran after a ladder, pushed it up the tree, and let it down into the hole.

Tommy was wild to go down. It was difficult to climb to the hole, because it was so high up, but Tommy was brave. And he wasn't afraid to climb down into the dark hollow in the trunk. Annika watched him disappear and wondered if she would ever see him again. She peeked in through the crack.

"Annika," came Tommy's voice. "You can't imagine how wonderful it is here. You must come in too. It isn't the least bit dangerous when you have a ladder to climb on. If you only do it once, you'll never want to do anything else."

"Are you sure?" asked Annika.

"Absolutely," said Tommy.

With trembling legs Annika climbed up in the tree again, and Pippi helped her with the last hard bit. She drew back a little when she saw how dark it was in the tree trunk, but Pippi held her hand and kept encouraging her.

"Don't be scared, Annika," she heard Tommy say from down below. "Now I can see your legs, and I'll certainly catch you if you fall."

But Annika didn't fall; she reached Tommy safely, and a moment later Pippi followed.

"Isn't it grand here?" said Tommy.

And Annika had to admit that it was. It wasn't nearly so dark as she had thought, because light came in through the crack. She peeked through and announced that she too could see the coffee pot outside on the grass.

"We'll have this for our secret hiding place," said Tommy. "Nobody will know that we are here. And if they should come and hunt around outside for us, we can see them through the crack. And we'll have a good laugh."

"We can have a little stick and poke it out through the crack and tickle them, and then they'll think the place is haunted," said Pippi.

At this idea the children were so delighted that they hugged each other, all three. They they heard the "ding-dong" that meant the bell was ringing for dinner at Tommy's and Annika's house.

"Oh, bother!" said Tommy. "Now we've got to go home. But we'll come over tomorrow as soon as we get back from school."

"Do that," said Pippi.

And so they climbed up the ladder, first Pippi, then Annika, and Tommy last. And then they climbed down out of the tree, first Pippi, then Annika, and Tommy last.

6

Pippi Arranges a Picnic

"WE don't have any school today because we're having Scrubbing Vacation," said Tommy to Pippi.

"Scrubbing Vacation? Well, I like that!" said Pippi. "Another injustice! Do I get any Scrubbing Vacation? Indeed I don't, though goodness knows I need one. Just look at the kitchen floor. But for that matter," she added, "now I come to think of it, I can scrub without any vacation. And that's what I intend to do right now, Scrubbing Vacation or no Scrubbing Vacation. I'd like to see anybody stop me! You two sit on the kitchen table, out of the way."

Tommy and Annika obediently climbed up on the kitchen table, and Mr. Nilsson hopped up after them and went to sleep in Annika's lap.

Pippi heated a big kettle of water and without
more ado poured it out on the kitchen floor. She took
off her big shoes and laid them neatly on the bread
plate. She tied two scrubbing brushes on her bare

feet and skated over the floor, plowing through the water so that it splashed all around her.

"I certainly should have been a skating princess," she said and kicked her left foot up so high that the scrubbing brush broke a piece out of the overhead light.

"Grace and charm I have at least," she continued and skipped nimbly over a chair standing in her way.

"Well, now I guess it's clean," she said at last and took off the brushes.

"Aren't you going to dry the floor?" asked Annika.

"Oh, no, it can dry in the sun," answered Pippi. "I don't think it will catch cold so long as it keeps moving."

Tommy and Annika climbed down from the table and stepped across the floor very carefully so they wouldn't get wet.

Out of doors the sun shone in a clear blue sky. It was one of those radiant September days that make you feel like walking in the woods. Pippi had an idea.

"Let's take Mr. Nilsson and go on a little picnic."

"Oh, yes, let's," cried Tommy and Annika.

"Run home and ask your mother then," said Pippi, "and I'll be getting the picnic basket ready."

Tommy and Annika thought that was a good suggestion. They rushed home and were back again almost immediately, but Pippi was already waiting by the gate with Mr. Nilsson on her shoulder, a walking stick in one hand, and a big basket in the other.

The children walked along the road a little way and then turned into a pasture where a pleasant path wound in and out among the thickets of birch and hazel. Presently they came to a gate on the other side of which was an even more beautiful pasture, but right in front of the gate stood a cow who looked as if nothing would persuade her to move. Annika yelled at her, and Tommy bravely went up and tried to push her away, but she just stood there staring at the children with her big cow eyes. To put an end to the matter, Pippi set down her basket and lifted the cow out of the way. The cow, looking very silly, lumbered off into the hazel bushes.

"Can you imagine that cows can be so bullheaded," said Pippi and jumped over the gate.

"What a lovely, lovely wood!" cried Annika in delight and climbed up on all the stones she could see. Tommy had brought along a dagger Pippi

had given him, and with it he cut walking sticks for
Annika and for himself. He cut his thumb a little
too, but that didn't matter.

"Maybe we ought to pick some mushrooms," said
Pippi, and she broke off a pretty, rosy one. "I wonder if it's possible to eat it?" she continued. "At any
rate, it isn't possible to drink it—that much I know;
so there is no choice except to eat it. Maybe its
possible."

She took a big bite and swallowed it. "It was possible," she announced, delighted. "Yes sirree, we'll
certainly stew the rest of this sometime," she said
and threw it high over the treetops.

"What have you got in your basket?" asked Annika. "Is it something good?"

"I wouldn't tell you for a thousand dollars," said
Pippi. "First we must find a good picnic spot."

The children began eagerly to look for such a
place. Annika found a large flat stone that she
thought was satisfactory, but it was covered with
red ants and "I don't want to sit with them," said
Pippi, "because I'm not acquainted with them."

"And besides, they bite," said Tommy.

"Do they?" said Pippi. "Bite back then."

Then Tommy found a little clearing among the

hazel bushes, and he thought that would be a good place.

"Oh, no, that's not sunny enough for my freckles," said Pippi, "and I do think freckles are so attractive."

Farther on they came to a hill that was easy to climb. On one side of the hill was a nice sunny rock just like a little balcony, and there they sat down.

"Now shut your eyes while I set the table," said Pippi. Tommy and Annika squeezed their eyes as tightly shut as possible. They heard Pippi opening the basket and rattling paper.

"One, two, nineteen—now you may look," said Pippi at last.

They looked, and they squealed with delight when they saw all the good things Pippi had spread on the bare rock. There were good sandwiches with meatballs and ham, a whole pile of sugared pancakes, several little brown sausages, and three pineapple puddings. For, you see, Pippi had learned cooking from the cook on her father's ship.

"Aren't Scrubbing Vacations grand?" said Tommy with his mouth full of pancakes. "We ought to have them every day."

"No, indeed, I'm not so crazy as all that to

scrub," said Pippi. "It's fun, to be sure, but not every day. That would be too tiresome."

At last the children were so full they could hardly move, and they sat still in the sunshine and just enjoyed it.

"I wonder if it is hard to fly," said Pippi and looked dreamily over the edge of the rock. The rock sloped down very steeply below them, and it was a long way to the ground.

"Down at least one ought to be able to learn to fly," she continued. "It must be harder to fly up. But you could begin with the easiest way. I do think I'll try."

"No, Pippi," cried both Tommy and Annika. "Oh, dear, Pippi, don't do that!"

But Pippi was already standing at the edge.

"Fly, you foolish fly, fly, and the foolish fly flew," she said, and just as she said "flew" she lifted her arms and took off into the air. In half a second there was a thud. It was Pippi hitting the ground. Tommy and Annika lay on their stomachs and looked down at her, terrified.

Pippi got up and brushed off her knees. "I forgot to flap," she said joyfully, "and I guess I had too many pancakes in my stomach."

At that moment the children noticed that Mr. Nilsson had disappeared. He had evidently gone off on a little expedition of his own. They remembered that they had last seen him contentedly chewing the picnic basket to pieces, but during Pippi's flying experiment they had forgotten him. And now he was gone.

Pippi was so angry that she threw her shoe into a big deep pool of water. "You should never take monkeys with you anywhere," she said. "He should have been left at home to pick fleas off the horse. That would have served him right," she continued, wading out into the pool to get her shoe. The water reached up to her waist.

"I might as well take advantage of this and wash my hair," said Pippi and ducked her head under the water and kept it there so long that the water began to bubble.

"There now, I've saved a visit to the hairdresser," she said contentedly when at last she came up for air. She stepped out of the pool and put on her shoe. Then they went off to hunt for Mr. Nilsson.

"Hear how it squishes when I walk," laughed Pippi. "It says 'klafs, klafs' in my dress and 'squish, squish' in my shoes. Isn't that jolly? I think you ought to try it too," she said to Annika, who was walking along beside her, with her lovely flaxen hair, pink dress, and little white kid shoes.

"Some other time," said the sensible Annika.

They walked on.

"Mr. Nilsson certainly can be aggravating," said Pippi. "He's always doing things like this. Once in Arabia he ran away from me and took a position as a maidservant to an elderly widow. That last was a lie, of course," she added after a pause.

Tommy suggested that they should all three go in different directions and hunt. At first Annika didn't want to because she was a little afraid, but Tommy said, "You aren't a 'fraidy cat, are you?" And, of course, Annika couldn't tolerate such an insult, so off they all went.

Tommy went through a field. Mr. Nilsson he did not find, but he did find something else. A bull! Or to be more exact, the bull found Tommy. And the bull did not like Tommy, for he was a very cross bull who was not at all fond of children. With his head down he charged toward Tommy, bellowing fearfully. Tommy let out a terrified shriek that could be heard all through the woods. Pippi and Annika heard it and came running to see what was the matter. By that time the bull had almost reached Tommy who had tumbled head over heels over a stump.

"What a stupid bull!" said Pippi to Annika, who was crying uncontrollably. "He ought to know he can't act like that. He'll get Tommy's white sailor suit all dirty. I'll have to go and talk some sense into the stupid animal."

And off she started. She ran up and pulled the bull by the tail. "Forgive me for breaking up the party," she said, and as she had given his tail a good hard pull the bull turned around and saw a new child to catch on his horns.

"As I was saying," went on Pippi, "forgive me for breaking up, and also forgive me for breaking off," and with that she broke off one of the bull's horns. "It isn't the style to have two horns this year," she said. "All the better bulls have just one horn—if any." And she broke off the other horn too.

As bulls have no feeling in their horns, this one didn't know what she had done. He charged at Pippi, and if she had been any other child there would have been nothing left but a grease spot.

"Hey, hey, stop tickling me!" shrieked Pippi. "You can't imagine how ticklish I am! Hey, stop, stop, or I'll die laughing!"

But the bull didn't stop, and at last Pippi jumped up on his back to get a little rest. To be sure, she didn't get much, because the bull didn't in the least approve of having Pippi on his back. He dodged about madly to get her off, but she clamped her knees and hung on. The bull dashed up and down the field, bellowing so hard that smoke came out of his nostrils. Pippi laughed and shrieked and waved at Tommy and Annika, who stood a little distance away, trembling like aspen leaves. The bull whirled round and round, trying to throw Pippi.

"See me dancing with my little friend!" cried Pippi and kept her seat. At last the bull was so tired that he lay down on the ground and wished that he'd never seen such a thing as a child. He had never thought children amounted to much anyway.

"Are you going to take a little nap now?" asked Pippi politely. "Then I won't disturb you."

She got off his back and went over to Tommy and Annika. Tommy had cried a little. He had a cut on one arm, but Annika had bandaged it with her handkerchief so that it no longer hurt.

"Oh, Pippi!" cried Annika excitedly.

"Sh, sh," whispered Pippi. "Don't wake the bull. He's sleeping. If we wake him he'll be fussy."

But the next minute, without paying any attention to the bull and his nap, she was shrieking at the top of her voice, "Mr. Nilsson, Mr. Nilsson, where are you? We've got to go home."

And, believe it or not, there sat Mr. Nilsson up in a pine tree, sucking his tail and looking so lonesome. It wasn't much fun for a little monkey to be left all alone in the woods. He skipped down from the pine and up on Pippi's shoulder, waving his little straw hat as he always did when he was very happy.

"Well, well, so you aren't going to be a maidservant this time?" said Pippi, stroking his back. "Oh, that was a lie, that's true," she continued. "But still, if it's true, how can it be a lie?" she argued. "You wait and see, it's going to turn out that he was a maidservant in Arabia after all, and if that's the case, I know who's going to make the meatballs at our house hereafter!"

And then they strolled home, Pippi's dress still going "klafs, klafs," and her shoes "squish, squish."

Tommy and Annika thought they had had a wonderful day in spite of the bull, and they sang a song they had learned at school. It was really a summer song, but they thought it fitted very well even if it was now nearly autumn:

"In the jolly summertime
Through field and wood we make our way.
Nobody's sad, everyone's gay.
We sing as we go, hol-lá, hol-ló!

You who are young,
Come join in our song.
Don't sit home moping all the day long.
Our song will swell
Through wood and dell
And up to the mountaintop as well.
In the jolly summertime
We sing as we go, hol-lá, hol-ló."

Pippi sang too, but with slightly different words:

"In the jolly summertime
Through field and wood I make my way.
I do exactly as I wish,
And when I walk it goes squish, squish,
Squish, squish. Squish, squish.

And my old shoe—
It's really true—
Sometimes says 'chip' and sometimes 'choo.'

For the shoe is wet.
The bull sleeps yet.
And I eat all the rice porridge I can get.
In the jolly summertime
I squish wherever I go. Squish-oh! Squish-oh!"

7

Pippi Goes
to the Circus

A CIRCUS had come to the little town, and all the children were begging their mothers and fathers for permission to go. Of course Tommy and Annika asked to go too, and their kind father immediately gave them some money.

Clutching it tightly in their hands, they rushed over to Pippi's. She was on the porch with her horse, braiding his tail into tiny pigtails and tying each one with red ribbon.

"I think it's his birthday today," she announced, "so he has to be all dressed up."

"Pippi," said Tommy, all out of breath because they had been running so fast, "Pippi, do you want to go with us to the circus?"

"I can go with you most anywhere," answered Pippi, "but whether I can go to the surkus or not I don't know, because I don't know what a surkus is. Does it hurt?"

"Silly!" said Tommy, "of course it doesn't hurt; it's fun. Horses and clowns and pretty ladies that walk the tightrope."

"But it costs money," said Annika, opening her small fist to see if the shiny half-dollar and the quarters were still there.

"I'm rich as a troll," said Pippi, "so I guess I can buy a surkus all right. But it'll be crowded here if I have more horses. The clowns and the pretty ladies I could keep in the laundry, but it's harder to know what to do with the horses."

"Oh, don't be so silly," said Tommy, "you don't buy a circus. It costs money to go and look at it—see?"

"Preserve us!" cried Pippi and shut her eyes tightly. "It costs money to *look?* And here I go around goggling all day long. Goodness knows how much money I've goggled up already!"

Then, little by little, she opened one eye very carefully, and it rolled round and round in her head. "Cost what it may," she said, "I must take a look!"

At last Tommy and Annika managed to explain to Pippi what a circus really was, and she took some gold pieces out of her suitcase. Then she put on her hat, which was as big as a millstone, and off they all went.

There were crowds of people outside the circus tent and a long line at the ticket window. But at last it was Pippi's turn. She stuck her head through the window and stared at the dear old lady sitting there.

"How much does it cost to look at you?" Pippi asked.

But the old lady was a foreigner who did not understand what Pippi meant and answered in broken Swedish.

"Little girl, it costs a dollar and a quarter in the grandstand and seventy-five cents on the benches and twenty-five cents for standing room."

Now Tommy interrupted and said that Pippi wanted a seventy-five-cent ticket. Pippi put down a gold piece and the old lady looked suspiciously at it. She bit it too, to see if it was genuine. At last she was convinced that it really was gold and gave Pippi her ticket and a great deal of change in silver.

"What would I do with all those nasty little white coins?" asked Pippi disgustedly. "Keep them and then I can look at you twice. In the standing room."

As Pippi absolutely refused to accept any change, the lady changed her ticket to one for the grand-stand and gave Tommy and Annika grandstand tickets too without their having to pay a single penny. In that way Pippi, Tommy, and Annika came to sit on some beautiful red chairs right next to the ring. Tommy and Annika turned around several times to wave to their schoolmates, who were sitting much farther away.

"This is a remarkable place," said Pippi, looking around in astonishment. "But, see, they've spilled sawdust all over the floor! Not that I'm overfussy myself, but that does look careless to me."

Tommy explained that all circuses had sawdust on the floor for the horses to run around in.

On a platform nearby the circus band suddenly began to play a thundering march. Pippi clapped her hands wildly and jumped up and down with delight.

"Does it cost money to hear too?" she asked, "or can you do that for nothing?"

At that moment the curtain in front of the per-formers' entrance was drawn aside, and the ring-master in a black frock coat, with a whip in his hand, came running in, followed by ten white horses with red plumes on their heads.

The ringmaster cracked his whip, and all the horses galloped around the ring. Then he cracked it again, and all the horses stood still with their front feet up on the railing around the ring.

One of them had stopped directly in front of the children. Annika didn't like to have a horse so near her and drew back in her chair as far as she could, but Pippi leaned forward and took the horse's right foot in her hands.

"Hello, there," she said, "my horse sent you his best wishes. It's his birthday today too, but he has bows on his tail instead of on his head."

Luckily she dropped the foot before the ringmaster cracked his whip again, because then all the horses jumped away from the railing and began to run around the ring.

When the number was over, the ringmaster bowed politely and the horses ran out. In an instant the curtain opened again for a coal-black horse. On its back stood a beautiful lady dressed in green silk tights. The program said her name was Miss Carmencita.

The horse trotted around in the sawdust, and Miss

Carmencita stood calmly on his back and smiled. But then something happened; just as the horse passed Pippi's seat, something came swishing through the air—and it was none other than Pippi herself. And there she stood on the horse's back, behind Miss Carmencita. At first Miss Carmencita was so astonished that she nearly fell off the horse. Then she got mad. She began to strike out with her hands behind her back to make Pippi jump off. But that didn't work.

"Take it easy," said Pippi. "Do you think you're the only one who can have any fun? Other people have paid too, haven't they?"

Then Miss Carmencita tried to jump off herself, but that didn't work either, because Pippi was holding her tightly around the waist. At that the audience couldn't help laughing. They thought it was so funny to see the lovely Miss Carmencita held against her will by a little red-headed youngster who stood there on the horse's back in her enormous shoes and looked as if she had never done anything except perform in a circus.

But the ringmaster didn't laugh. He turned toward an attendant in a red uniform and made a sign to him to go and stop the horse.

"Is this number already over," asked Pippi in a

disappointed tone, "just when we were having so much fun?"

"Horrible child!" hissed the ringmaster between his teeth. "Get out of here!"

Pippi looked at him sadly. "Why are you mad at me?" she asked. "What's the matter? I thought we were here to have fun."

She skipped off the horse and went back to her seat. But now two huge guards came to throw her out. They took hold of her and tried to lift her up.

They couldn't do it. Pippi sat absolutely still, and it was impossible to budge her although they tried as hard as they could. At last they shrugged their shoulders and went off.

Meanwhile the next number had begun. It was Miss Elvira about to walk the tightrope. She wore a pink tulle skirt and carried a pink parasol in her hand. With delicate little steps she ran out on the rope. She swung her legs gracefully in the air and did all sorts of tricks. It looked so pretty. She even showed how she could walk backward on the narrow rope. But when she got back to the little platform at the end of the rope, there stood Pippi.

"What are you going to do now?" asked Pippi,

delighted when she saw how astonished Miss Elvira looked.

Miss Elvira said nothing at all but jumped down from the rope and threw her arms around the ringmaster's neck, for he was her father. And the ringmaster once more sent for his guards to throw Pippi out. This time he sent for five of them, but all the people shouted, "Let her stay! We want to see the red-headed girl." And they stamped their feet and clapped their hands.

Pippi ran out on the rope; and Miss Elvira's tricks were as nothing compared with Pippi's. When she got to the middle of the rope she stretched one leg straight up in the air, and her big shoe spread out like a roof over her head. She bent her foot a little so that she could tickle herself with it back of her ear.

The ringmaster was not at all pleased to have Pippi performing in his circus. He wanted to get rid of her, and so he stole up and loosened the mechanism that held the rope taut, thinking surely Pippi would fall down.

But Pippi didn't. She set the rope a-swinging instead. Back and forth it swayed, and Pippi swung faster and faster, until suddenly she leaped out into

the air and landed right on the ringmaster. He was
so frightened he began to run.

"Oh, what a jolly horse!" cried Pippi. "But why
don't you have any pompoms in your hair?"

Now Pippi decided it was time to go back to
Tommy and Annika. She jumped off the ringmaster
and went back to her seat. The next number was
about to begin, but there was a brief pause because
the ringmaster had to go out and get a drink of water
and comb his hair.

Then he came in again, bowed to the audience, and
said, "Ladies and gentlemen, in a moment you will
be privileged to see the Greatest Marvel of all time,
the Strongest Man in the World, the Mighty Adolf,
whom no one has yet been able to conquer. Here he
comes, ladies and gentlemen, Allow me to present to
you THE MIGHTY ADOLF."

And into the ring stepped a man who looked as big
as a giant. He wore flesh-colored tights and had a
leopard skin draped around his stomach. He bowed
to the audience and looked very pleased with himself.

"Look at these muscles," said the ringmaster and
squeezed the Mighty Adolf's arm where the muscles
stood out like balls under the skin.

"And now, ladies and gentlemen, I have a very special invitation for you. Who will challenge the Mighty Adolf in a wrestling match? Who of you dares to try his strength against the World's Strongest Man? A hundred dollars for anyone who can conquer the Mighty Adolf! A hundred dollars, ladies and gentlemen! Think of that! Who will be the first to try?"

Nobody came forth.

"What did he say?" asked Pippi.

"He says that anybody who can lick that big man will get a hundred dollars," answered Tommy.

"I can," said Pippi, "but I think it's too bad to, because he looks nice."

"Oh, no, you couldn't," said Annika, "he's the strongest man in the world."

"*Man,* yes," said Pippi, "but I am the strongest girl in the world, remember that."

Meanwhile the Mighty Adolf was lifting heavy iron weights and bending thick iron rods in the middle just to show how strong he was.

"Oh, come now, ladies and gentlemen," cried the ringmaster, "is there really nobody here who wants to earn a hundred dollars? Shall I really be forced to keep this myself?" And he waved a bill in the air.

"No, that you certainly won't be forced to do," said Pippi and stepped over the railing into the ring.

The ringmaster was absolutely wild when he saw her. "Get out of here! I don't want to see any more of you," he hissed.

"Why do you always have to be so unfriendly?" said Pippi reproachfully. "I just want to fight with Mighty Adolf."

"This is no place for jokes," said the ringmaster. "Get out of here before the Mighty Adolf hears your impudent nonsense."

But Pippi went right by the ringleader and up to Mighty Adolf. She took his hand and shook it heartily.

"Shall we fight a little, you and I?" she asked.

Mighty Adolf looked at her but didn't understand a word.

"In one minute I'll begin," said Pippi.

And begin she did. She grabbed Mighty Adolf around the waist, and before anyone knew what was happening she had thrown him on the mat. Mighty Adolf leaped up, his face absolutely scarlet.

"Atta girl, Pippi!" shrieked Tommy and Annika, so loudly that all the people at the circus heard it and began to shriek "Atta girl, Pippi!" too. The ringmaster sat on the railing, wringing his hands. He was mad, but Mighty Adolf was madder. Never in his life had he experienced anything so humiliating as this. And he certainly intended to show that red-headed girl what kind of a man Mighty Adolf really was. He rushed at Pippi and caught her round the waist, but Pippi stood firm as a rock.

"You can do better than that," she said to encourage him. Then she wriggled out of his grasp, and in the twinkling of an eye Mighty Adolf was on the mat again. Pippi stood beside him, waiting. She didn't have to wait long. With a roar he was up again, rushing at her.

"Tiddelipom and piddeliday," said Pippi.

All the people in the tent stamped their feet and threw their hats in the air and shouted, "Hurrah, Pippi!"

When Mighty Adolf came rushing at her for the third time, Pippi lifted him high in the air and, with her arms straight above her, carried him clear around the ring. Then she laid him down on the mat again and held him there.

"Now, little fellow," said she, "I don't think we'll bother about this any more. We'll never have any more fun than we've had already."

"Pippi is the winner! Pippi is the winner!" cried all the people.

Mighty Adolf stole out as fast as he could, and the ringmaster had to go up and hand Pippi the hundred dollars, although he looked as if he'd much prefer to eat her.

"Here you are, young lady, here you are," said he. "One hundred dollars."

"That thing!" said Pippi scornfully. "What would I want with that old piece of paper. Take it and use it to fry herring on if you want to." And she went back to her seat.

"This is certainly a long surkus," she said to Tommy and Annika. "I think I'll take a little snooze, but wake me if they need my help about anything else."

And then she lay back in her chair and went to sleep at once. There she lay and snored while the clowns, the sword swallowers, and the snake charmers did their tricks for Tommy and Annika and all the rest of the people at the circus.

"Just the same, I think Pippi was best of all," whispered Tommy to Annika.

8.
Pippi
Entertains
Two Burglars

AFTER Pippi's performance at the circus there was not a single person in all the little town who did not know how strong she was. There was even a piece about her in the paper. But people who lived in other places, of course, didn't know who Pippi was.

One dark autumn evening two tramps came walking down the road past Villa Villekulla. They were two bad thieves wandering about the country to see what they could steal. They saw that there was a light in the windows of Villa Villekulla and decided to go in to ask for a sandwich.

That evening Pippi had poured out all her gold pieces on the kitchen floor and sat there counting them. To be sure, she couldn't count very well, but she did it now and then anyway, just to keep everything in order.

". . . sixty-five, sixty-six, sixty-seven, sixty-eight, sixty-nine, sixty-ten, sixty-eleven, sixty-twelve, sixty-thirteen, sixty-sixteen—whew, it makes my throat feel like sixty! Goodness, there must be *some* more numbers in the arithmetic; oh, yes, now I remember—one hundred four, one thousand. That certainly is a lot of money," said Pippi.

There was a loud knock on the door.

"Walk in or stay out, whichever you choose!" shouted Pippi. "I never force anyone against his will."

The door opened and the two tramps came in. You can imagine that they opened their eyes when they saw a little red-haired girl sitting all alone on the floor, counting money.

"Are you all alone at home?" they asked craftily.

"Of course not," said Pippi. "Mr. Nilsson is at home too."

The thieves couldn't very well know that Mr. Nilsson was a monkey sleeping in a little green bed with a doll's quilt around his stomach. They thought the man of the house must be named Mr. Nilsson and they winked at each other. "We can come back a little later" is what they meant, but to Pippi they said, "We just came in to ask what your clock is."

They were so excited that they had forgotten all about the sandwich.

"Great, strong men who don't know what a clock is!" said Pippi. "Where in the world were you brought up? The clock is a little round thingamajig that says 'tick tack, tick tack,' and that goes and goes but never gets to the door. Do you know any more riddles? Out with them if you do," said Pippi encouragingly.

The tramps thought Pippi was too little to tell time, so without another word they went out again.

"I don't demand that you say 'tack' " (thanks in Swedish), shouted Pippi after them, "but you could at least make an effort and say 'tick.' You haven't even as much sense as a clock has. But by all means go in peace." And Pippi went back to her counting.

No sooner were the tramps outside than they began to rub their hands with delight. "Did you see all that money? Heavenly day!" said one of them.

"Yes, once in a while luck is with us," said the other. "All we need to do is wait until the kid and that Nilsson are asleep. Then we'll sneak in and bag the lot."

They sat down under an oak tree in the garden to wait. A drizzling rain was falling; they were very hungry, so they were quite uncomfortable, but the thought of all that money kept their spirits up.

From time to time lights went out in other houses, but in Villa Villekulla they shone on. It so happened that Pippi was learning to dance the schottische, and she didn't want to go to bed until she was sure she could do it. At last, however, the lights went out in the windows of Villa Villekulla too.

The tramps waited quite a while until they were sure Mr. Nilsson must have gone to sleep. At last they crept quietly up to the kitchen door and prepared to open it with their burglar tools. Meanwhile one of them—his name, as a matter of fact, was Bloom—just happened to feel of the doorknob. The door was not locked!

"Well, some people *are* smart!" he whispered to his companion. "The door is open!"

"So much the better for us," answered his companion, a black-haired man called Thunder-Karlsson by those who knew him. Thunder-Karlsson lighted his pocket torch, and they crept into the kitchen. There was no one there. In the next room was Pippi's bed, and there also stood Mr. Nilsson's little doll bed.

Thunder-Karlsson opened the door and looked around carefully. Everything was quiet as he played his torch around the room. When the light touched Pippi's bed the two tramps were amazed to see nothing but a pair of feet on the pillow. Pippi, as usual, had her head under the covers at the foot of the bed.

"That must be the girl," whispered Thunder-Karlsson to Bloom. "And no doubt she sleeps soundly. But where in the world is Nilsson, do you suppose?"

"*Mr.* Nilsson, if you please," came Pippi's calm voice from under the covers. "*Mr.* Nilsson is in the little green doll bed."

The tramps were so startled that they almost rushed out at once, but then it suddenly dawned on them what Pippi had said. That Mr. Nilsson was lying in a *doll's* bed! And now in the light of the torch they could see the little bed and the tiny monkey lying in it.

Thunder-Karlsson   couldn't   help   laughing.

"Bloom," he said, "Mr. Nilsson is a monkey. Can you beat that?"

"Well, what did you think he was?" came Pippi's calm voice from under the covers again. "A lawn mower?"

"Aren't your mother and father at home?" asked Bloom.

"No," said Pippi. "They're gone. Completely gone."

Thunder-Karlsson and Bloom chuckled with delight.

"Listen, little girl," said Thunder-Karlsson, "come out so we can talk to you."

"No, I'm sleeping," said Pippi. "Is it more riddles you want? If so, answer this one. What is it that goes and goes and never gets to the door?"

Now Bloom went over and pulled the covers off Pippi.

"Can you dance the schottische?" asked Pippi, looking him gravely in the eye. "I can."

"You ask too many questions," said Thunder-Karlsson. "Can't we ask a few too? Where, for instance, is the money you had on the floor a little while ago?"

"In the suitcase on top of the wardrobe," answered Pippi truthfully.

Thunder-Karlsson and Bloom grinned.

"I hope you don't have anything against our taking it, little friend," said Thunder-Karlsson.

"Certainly not," said Pippi. "Of course I don't."

Whereupon Bloom lifted down the suitcase.

"I hope you don't have anything against my taking it back, little friend," said Pippi, getting out of bed and stepping over to Bloom.

Bloom had no idea how it all happened, but suddenly the suitcase was in Pippi's hand.

"Here, quit your fooling!" said Thunder-Karlsson angrily. "Hand over the suitcase." He took Pippi firmly by the hand and tried to snatch back the booty.

"Fooling, fooling, too much fooling," said Pippi and lifted Thunder-Karlsson up on the wardrobe. A moment later she had Bloom up there too. Then the tramps were frightened; they began to see that Pippi was no ordinary girl. However, the suitcase tempted them so much they forgot their fright.

"Come on now, both together," yelled Thunder-Karlsson, and they jumped down from the wardrobe and threw themselves on Pippi, who had the suitcase in her hand. Pippi gave each one a little poke with her finger, and they shrank away into a corner. Before they had a chance to get up again, Pippi had fetched a rope and quick as a flash had bound the arms and legs of both burglars. Now they sang a different tune.

"Please, please, miss," begged Thunder-Karlsson, "forgive us. We were only joking. Don't hurt us. We are just two tramps who came in to ask for food."

Bloom even began to cry a bit.

Pippi put the suitcase neatly back on the wardrobe. Then she turned to her prisoners. "Can either of you dance the schottische?"

"Why, yes," said Thunder-Karlsson, "I guess we both can."

"Oh, what fun!" cried Pippi, clapping her hands "Can't we dance a little? I've just learned, you know."

"Well, certainly, by all means," said Thunder-Karlsson, a bit confused.

Pippi took some large scissors and cut the ropes that bound her guests.

"But we don't have any music," she said in a

worried voice. Then she had an idea. "Can't you blow on a comb?" she said to Bloom. "And I'll dance with him." She pointed to Thunder-Karlsson.

Oh, yes, Bloom could blow on a comb, all right. And blow he did, so that you could hear it all through the house. Mr. Nilsson sat up in bed, wide awake, just in time to see Pippi whirling around with Thunder-Karlsson. She was dead serious and danced as if her life depended on it.

At last Bloom said he couldn't blow on the comb any longer because it tickled his mouth unmercifully. And Thunder-Karlsson, who had tramped the roads all day, began to feel tired.

"Oh, please, just a little longer," begged Pippi, dancing on, and Bloom and Thunder-Karlsson could do nothing but continue.

At three in the morning Pippi said, "I could keep on dancing until Thursday, but maybe you're tired and hungry."

That was exactly what they were, though they hardly dared to say so. Pippi went to the pantry and took out bread and cheese and butter, ham and cold roast and milk; and they sat around the kitchen table—Bloom and Thunder-Karlsson, and Pippi—and ate until they were almost four-cornered.

Pippi poured a little milk into her ear. "That's good for earache," she said.

"Poor thing, have you got an earache?" asked Bloom.

"No," said Pippi, "but I might get one."

Finally the two tramps got up, thanked Pippi for the food, and begged to be allowed to say good-by.

"It was awfully jolly that you came. Do you really have to go so soon?" said Pippi regretfully. "Never have I seen anyone who can dance the schottische the way you do, my sugar pig," she said to Thunder-Karlsson. And to Bloom, "If you keep on practicing on the comb, you won't notice the tickling."

As they were going out of the door Pippi came running after them and gave them each a gold piece. "These you have honestly earned," she said.

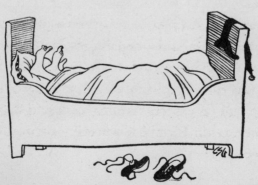

Pippi Goes to a Coffee Party

Tommy's and Annika's mother had invited a few ladies to a coffee party, and as she had done plenty of baking she thought Tommy and Annika might invite Pippi over at the same time. The children would entertain each other and give no trouble to anyone.

Tommy and Annika were overjoyed when their mother told them and immediately dashed over to Pippi's to invite her. Pippi was in the garden, watering the few flowers still in bloom with an old rusty watering can. As it was raining cats and dogs that day Tommy told Pippi her watering seemed hardly necessary.

"Yes, that's what you say," said Pippi grudgingly, "but I've lain awake all night thinking what fun it was going to be to get up and water, and I'm not going to let a little rain stand in my way."

Now Annika came forth with the delightful news about the coffee party.

"A coffee party! *Me!*" cried Pippi, and she was so excited that she began to water Tommy instead of the rosebush she intended to sprinkle. "Oh, what will happen? Oh, I'm so nervous. What if I can't behave myself?"

"Of course you can," said Annika.

"Don't you be too certain about that," said Pippi. "You can be sure I'll try, but I have noticed several times that people don't think I know how to behave even when I'm trying as hard as ever I can. At sea we were never so fussy about things like that. But I promise that I'll take special pains today so you won't have to be ashamed of me."

"Good," said Tommy, and he and Annika hurried home again in the rain.

"This afternoon at three o'clock, don't forget," cried Annika, peeking out from under the umbrella.

At three o'clock a very stylish young lady walked

up the steps of the Settergrens' house. It was Pippi Longstocking. For this special occasion she had unbraided her pigtails, and her red hair hung like a lion's mane around her. With red crayon she had painted her mouth fiery red, and she had blackened her eyebrows so that she looked almost dangerous. With the crayon she had also painted her fingernails, and she had put big green rosettes on her shoes.

"I should imagine I'll be the most stylish person of all at this party," she said contentedly to herself as she rang the doorbell.

In the Settergrens' living room sat three fine ladies, and with them Tommy, Annika, and their mother. A wonderful coffee table had been spread, and in the fireplace a fire was burning brightly. The ladies were talking quietly with one another, and Tommy and Annika were sitting on the sofa, looking at an album. Everything was so peaceful.

Suddenly the peace was shattered.

"Atten–shun!" A piercing cry came from the hall, and the next minute Pippi Longstocking stood in the doorway. She had cried out so loudly and so unexpectedly that the ladies had jumped in their seats.

"Forward march!" came the next command, and Pippi, with measured steps, walked up to Mrs. Settergren.

"Halt!" She stopped. "Arms forward, one, *two*," she cried and with both hands gripped one of Mrs. Settergren's and shook it heartily.

"Knees bend!" she shrieked and curtsied prettily. Then she smiled at Mrs. Settergren and said in her ordinary voice, "You see, I am really very shy, so if I didn't give myself some commands I'd just stand in the hall and not dare to come in."

Then she rushed up to the other ladies and kissed them on the cheek.

"Charming, charming, upon my honor!" said she, for she had once heard a stylish gentleman say that to a lady. Then she sat down in the best chair she could find. Mrs. Settergren had intended the children to have their party up in Tommy's and Annika's room, but Pippi stayed calmly in her chair, slapped herself on the knee, and said, looking at the coffee table, "That certainly looks good. When do we begin?"

At that moment Ella, the maid, came in with the coffee pot, and Mrs. Settergren said, "Please come and have some coffee."

"First!" cried Pippi and was up by the table in two skips. She heaped as many cakes as she could onto a plate, threw five lumps of sugar into a coffee cup, emptied half the cream pitcher into her cup, and was back in her chair with her loot even before the ladies had reached the table.

Pippi stretched her legs out in front of her and placed the plate of cakes between her toes. Then she merrily dunked cakes in her coffee cup and stuffed so many in her mouth at once that she couldn't have uttered a word no matter how hard she tried. In the twinkling of an eye she had finished all the cakes on the plate. She got up, struck the plate as if it were a tambourine, and went up to the table to see if there were any cakes left. The ladies looked disapprovingly at her, but that didn't bother her. Chatting gaily, she walked around the table, snatching a cake here and a cake there.

"It certainly was nice of you to invite me," she said. "I've never been to a coffee party before."

On the table stood a large cream pie, decorated in the center with a piece of red candy. Pippi stood with her hands behind her back and looked at it. Suddenly she bent down and snatched the candy with her teeth. But she dived down a little too hastily, and when she came up again her whole face was covered with whipped cream.

"Goody!" laughed Pippi. "Now we can play blindman's buff, for we've certainly got a blind man all made to order! I can't see a thing!"

She stuck out her tongue and licked away the cream. "This was indeed a dreadful accident," said she. "And the pie is all ruined now anyway, so I may as well eat it all up at once."

She dug into it with the pie server, and in a few minutes the whole pie had disappeared. Pippi patted her stomach contentedly. Mrs. Settergren had gone out into the kitchen so she knew nothing about the accident to the cream pie, but the other ladies looked very sternly at Pippi. No doubt they would have liked a little pie too. Pippi noticed that they looked disappointed and decided to cheer them up.

"Now you mustn't feel bad about such a little accident," she said comfortingly. "The main thing is that we have our health. And at a coffee party you should have fun."

She then picked up a sugar bowl and tipped all the lump sugar in it out on the floor. "Well, my goodness!" she cried. "Now look what I've done! How could I make such a mistake? I thought this

was the granulated sugar. Bad luck seems to follow
me today."

Thereupon she took a sugar spoon out of another
bowl and began to sprinkle granulated sugar all over
the floor. "I hope you notice," she said, "that this is
the kind of sugar you sprinkle on things. So it's
perfectly all right for me to do this. Because why
should there be the kind of sugar to sprinkle on
things if somebody doesn't go and sprinkle it?—
that's what I'd like to know.

"Have you ever noticed what fun it is to walk on
a floor that has had sugar sprinkled all over it?" she
asked the ladies. "Of course it's even more fun when
you're barefoot," she added as she pulled off her
shoes and stockings. "You ought to try it too, because nothing's more fun, believe me!"

At that moment Mrs. Settergren came in, and
when she saw the sugar all over the floor she took
Pippi firmly by the arm and led her over to the sofa
to Tommy and Annika. Then she went over to the
ladies and invited them to have more coffee. That
the cream pie had disappeared only made her happy,
because she thought the ladies had liked it so much
that they had eaten it all.

Pippi, Tommy, and Annika sat talking quietly on

the sofa. The fire crackled on the hearth. The ladies drank their coffee, and all was quiet and peaceful again. And as so often happens at coffee parties, the ladies began to talk about their servant problems. Apparently they had not been able to get very good servants, for they were not at all satisfied with them, and they agreed that it really was better not to have any servants at all. It was much more satisfactory to do things yourself because then you at least knew that things were done right.

Pippi sat on the sofa listening, and after the ladies had been talking a while she said, "Once my grandmother had a servant named Malin. She had chilblains on her feet, but otherwise there was nothing wrong with her. The only annoying thing was that as soon as company came she would rush at them and bite their legs. And bark! Oh, how she would bark! You could hear it all through the neighborhood, but it was only because she was playful. Only, of course, strangers didn't always understand that. The dean's wife, an elderly woman, came to see Grandmother once soon after Malin first came, and when Malin came dashing at her and bit her in the ankle, the dean's wife screamed so loudly that it scared Malin, so that her teeth clamped together and she couldn't get them apart. There she sat, stuck to the dean's wife's ankle until Friday. And Grandmother had to peel the potatoes herself. But at least it was well done. She peeled so well that when she was done there were no potatoes left—only peelings. But after that Friday the dean's wife never came to call on Grandmother again. She just never could take a joke. And poor Malin who was always so good-natured and happy! Though for that matter she was a little touchy at times, there's no denying that. Once when Grandmother poked a fork in her ear she howled all day."

Pippi looked around and smiled pleasantly. "Yes, that was Malin for you," she said and twiddled her thumbs.

The ladies acted as if they had heard nothing. They continued to talk.

"If my Rosa were only clean," said Mrs. Berggren, "then maybe I could keep her. But she's a regular pig—"

"Say, you ought to have seen Malin," Pippi interrupted. "Malin was so outrageously dirty that it was a joy to see her, Grandmother said. For the longest time Grandmother thought she had a very dark complexion but, honest and true, it was nothing but dirt that would wash off. And once at a bazaar at the City Hotel she got first prize for the dirt under her nails. Mercy me, how dirty that girl was!" said Pippi happily. Mrs. Settergren looked at her sternly.

"Can you imagine!" said Mrs. Granberg. "The other evening when Britta was going out she borrowed my blue satin dress without even asking for it. Isn't that dreadful?"

"Yes, indeed," said Pippi, "she certainly seems to be cut from the same piece of cloth as Malin, from what you say. Grandmother had a pink undershirt that she was specially fond of. But the worst of it was that Malin liked it too. And every morning Grandmother and Malin argued about who was to wear the undershirt. At last they decided it would be fair to take turns and each wear it every other day. But imagine how tricky Malin could be! Sometimes she'd come running in when it wasn't her turn at all and say, 'No mashed turnip today if I can't wear the pink woolen undershirt!' Well, what was Grandmother to do? Mashed turnip was her very favorite dish. There was nothing for it but to give

Malin the shirt. As soon as Malin got the shirt she
went out into the kitchen as nice as could be and began to mash turnip so that it spattered all over the
walls."

There was silence for a little while, and then Mrs.
Alexandersson said, "I'm not absolutely certain but
I strongly suspect that my Hulda steals. In fact I've
noticed that things disappear."

"Malin," began Pippi, but Mrs. Settergren interrupted her. "Children," she said decidedly, "go
up to the nursery immediately!"

"Yes, but I was only going to tell that Malin stole
too," said Pippi. "Like a raven! Everything she
could lay her hands on. She used to get up in the
middle of the night and steal; otherwise she couldn't
sleep well, she said. Once she stole Grandmother's
piano and tucked it into her own top bureau drawer.
She was very clever with her hands, Grandmother
said."

Tommy and Annika took hold of Pippi and
pulled her out of the room and up the stairs. The
ladies began on their third cups of coffee, and Mrs.
Settergren said, "It's not that I want to complain
about my Ella, but she does break the china."

A red head appeared over the stair rail.

"Speaking of Malin," said Pippi, "maybe you are wondering if she used to break any china. Well, she did. She set apart one day a week just to break china. It was Tuesday, Grandmother said. As early as five o'clock on Tuesday morning you could hear this jewel of a maid in the kitchen, breaking china. She began with the coffee cups and glasses and little things like that and then went on to the soup bowls and dinner plates, and she finished up with platters and soup tureens. There was such a crash bang in the kitchen all morning that it was a joy to hear it, Grandmother said. And if Malin had any spare time late in the afternoon, she would go into the drawing room with a little hammer and knock down the antique East Indian plates that were hanging on the walls. Grandmother bought new china every Wednesday," said Pippi and disappeared up the stairs as quickly as a jack-in-the-box.

But now Mrs. Settergren's patience had come to an end. She ran up the stairs, into the nursery, and up to Pippi, who had just begun to teach Tommy to stand on his head.

"You must never come here again," said Mrs. Settergren, "when you can't behave any better than this."

Pippi looked at her in astonishment and her eyes slowly filled with tears. "That's just what I was afraid of," she said. "That I couldn't behave properly. It's no use to try; I'll never learn. I should have stayed on the ocean."

She curtsied to Mrs. Settergren, said good-by to Tommy and Annika, and went slowly down the stairs.

The ladies were now getting ready to go home too. Pippi sat down in the hall near the shelf where rubbers were kept and watched the ladies putting on their hats and coats.

"Too bad you don't like your maids," said she. "You should have one like Malin. Grandmother always said there was nobody like her. Imagine! One Christmas when Malin was going to serve a little roast pig, do you know what she did? She had read in the cookbook that roast pig must be served with frilled paper in the ears and an apple in the mouth. But poor Malin didn't understand that it was the pig who was supposed to have the apple. You should have seen her when she came in on Christmas Eve with her best apron on and a big Gravenstein apple in her mouth. 'Oh, Malin, you're crazy!' Grandmother said to her, and Malin couldn't say a word in her own defense, she could only wiggle her ears until the frilled paper rustled. To be sure, she tried to say something, but it just sounded like blubb, blubb, blubb. And of course she couldn't bite people in the leg as she usually did, and it *would* be a day when there was a lot of company. Poor little Malin, it wasn't a very happy Christmas Eve for her," said Pippi sadly.

The ladies were now dressed and said a last good-by to Mrs. Settergren. And Pippi ran up to her and whispered, "Forgive me because I couldn't behave myself. Good-by!"

Then she put on her large hat and followed the ladies. Outside the gate their ways parted. Pippi went toward Villa Villekulla and the ladies in the other direction.

When they had gone a little way they heard someone panting behind them. It was Pippi who had come racing back.

"You can imagine that Grandmother mourned when she lost Malin. Just think, one Tuesday morning when Malin had had time to break only about a dozen teacups she ran away and went to sea. And

Grandmother had to break the china herself that day. She wasn't used to it, poor thing, and she got blisters all over her hands. She never saw Malin again. And that was a shame because she was such an excellent maid, Grandmother said."

Pippi left, and the ladies hurried on, but when they had gone a couple of hundred feet, they heard Pippi, from far off, yelling at the top of her lungs, "SHE NEVER SWEPT UNDER THE BEDS."

10.
Pippi Acts as a Lifesaver

ONE Sunday afternoon Pippi sat wondering what to do. Tommy and Annika had gone to a tea party with their mother and father, so she knew she couldn't expect a visit from them.

The day had been filled with pleasant tasks. She had got up early and served Mr. Nilsson fruit juice and buns in bed. He looked so cute sitting there in his light blue nightshirt, holding the glass in both hands. Then she had fed and groomed the horse and told him a long story of her adventures at sea. Next she had gone into the parlor and painted a large picture on the wallpaper. The picture represented a fat lady in a red dress and a black hat. In one hand she held a yellow flower and in the other a dead rat. Pippi thought it a very beautiful picture; it dressed up the whole room. Then she had sat down in front of her chest and looked at all her birds' eggs and shells, and thought about the wonderful places where she and her father had collected them, and about all the pleasant little shops all over the world where they had bought the beautiful things that were now in the drawers of her chest. Then she had tried to teach Mr. Nilsson to dance the schottische, but he didn't want to learn. For a while she had thought of trying to teach the horse, but instead she had crept down into the woodbox and pulled the cover down. She had pretended she was a sardine in a sardine box and, it was a shame Tommy and Annika weren't there so they could have been sardines too.

Now it had begun to grow dark. She pressed her little pug nose against the windowpane and looked out into the autumn dusk. She remembered that she hadn't been riding for a couple of days and decided to go at once. That would be a nice ending to a pleasant Sunday.

Accordingly she put on her big hat, fetched Mr. Nilsson from a corner where he sat playing marbles, saddled the horse, and lifted him down from the porch. And off they went, Mr. Nilsson on Pippi and Pippi on the horse.

It was quite cold and the roads were frozen, so there was a good crunchy sound as they rode along. Mr. Nilsson sat on Pippi's shoulder and tried to catch hold of some of the branches of the trees as they went by, but Pippi rode so fast that it was no use. Instead, the branches kept boxing him in the ears, and he had a hard time keeping his straw hat on his head.

Pippi rode through the little town, and people pressed anxiously up against the walls when she came storming by.

The town had a market square, of course. There were several charming old one-story buildings and a little yellow-painted town hall. And there was also an ugly wretch of a building, newly built and three stories high. It was called "The Skyscraper" because it was taller than any of the other houses in town.

On a Sunday afternoon the little town was always quiet and peaceful, but suddenly the quiet was broken by loud cries. "The Skyscraper's burning! Fire! Fire!"

People came running excitedly from all directions. The fire engine came clanging down the

street, and the little children who usually thought
fire engines were such fun now cried from fright
because they were sure their own houses would catch
fire too. The police had to hold back the crowds of
people gathering in the square so that the fire engine could get through. The flames came leaping out
of the windows of the Skyscraper, and smoke and
sparks enveloped the firemen who were courageously
trying to put out the fire. The fire had started on the
first floor but was quickly spreading to the upper
stories.

Suddenly the crowd saw a sight that made them
gasp with horror. At the top of the house was a
gable, and in the gable window, which a little child's
hand had just opened, stood two little boys calling
for help. "We can't get out because somebody has
built a fire on the stairs," cried the older boy.

He was five and his brother a year younger. Their
mother had gone out on an errand, and there they
stood, all alone. Many of the people in the square
began to cry, and the fire chief looked worried. There
was, of course, a ladder on the fire truck, but it
wouldn't reach anywhere near to the little boys. To
get into the house to save the children was impossible. A wave of despair swept over the crowd in

the square when they realized there was no way to help the children. And the poor little things just stood up there and cried. It wouldn't be long now before the fire reached the attic.

In the midst of the crowd in the square sat Pippi on her horse. She looked with great interest at the fire engine and wondered if she should buy one like it. She liked it because it was red and because it made such a fearful noise as it went through the streets. Then she looked at the fire and she thought it was fun when a few sparks fell on her.

Presently she noticed the little boys up in the attic. To her astonishment they looked as if they weren't enjoying the fire at all. That was more than she could understand and at last she had to ask the crowd around her, "Why are the children crying?"

First she got only sobs in answer, but finally a stout gentleman said, "Well, what do you think? Don't you suppose you'd cry yourself if you were up there and couldn't get down?"

"I never cry," said Pippi, "but if they want to get down, why doesn't somebody help them?"

"Because it isn't possible, of course," said the stout gentleman.

Pippi thought for a while. Then she asked, "Can anybody bring me a long rope?"

"What good would that do?" asked the stout gentleman. "The children are too small to get down the rope, and, for that matter, how would you ever get the rope up to them?"

"Oh, I've been around a bit," said Pippi calmly. "I want a rope."

There was not a single person who thought it would do any good, but somehow or other Pippi got her rope.

Not far from the gable of the Skyscraper grew a tall tree. The top of it was almost level with the attic window, but between the tree and the window was a distance of almost three yards. And the trunk of the tree was smooth and had no branches for climbing on. Even Pippi wouldn't be able to climb it.

The fire burned. The children in the window screamed. The people in the square cried.

Pippi jumped off the horse and went up to the tree. Then she took the rope and tied it tightly to Mr. Nilsson's tail.

"Now you be Pippi's good boy," she said. She put him on the tree trunk and gave him a little push.

He understood perfectly what he was supposed to do. And he climbed obediently up the tree trunk. Of course it was no trouble at all for a little monkey to do that.

The people in the square held their breath and watched Mr. Nilsson. Soon he had reached the top of the tree. There he sat on a branch and looked down at Pippi. She beckoned to him to come down again. He did so at once, climbing down on the other side of the branch, so that when he reached the ground the rope was looped over the branch and hung down double with both ends on the ground.

"Good for you, Mr. Nilsson," said Pippi. "You're so smart you can be a professor any time you wish." She untied the knot that had fastened the rope to Mr. Nilsson's tail.

Nearby, a house was being repaired, and Pippi ran over and got a long board. She took the board in one hand, ran to the tree, grasped the rope in her free hand, and braced her feet against the trunk of the tree. Quickly and nimbly she climbed up the trunk, and the people stopped crying in astonishment. When she reached the top of the tree she placed the board over a stout branch and then carefully pushed it over to the window sill. And there lay the board like a bridge between the top of the tree and the window.

The people down in the square stood absolutely silent. They were so tense they couldn't say a word. Pippi stepped out on the board. She smiled pleasantly at the two boys in the gabled window. "Why do you look so sad?" she asked. "Have you got a stomach-ache?"

She ran across the board and hopped in at the window. "My, it seems warm in here," she said. "You don't need to make any more fire in here today, that I can guarantee. And at the most four sticks in the stove tomorrow, I should think."

Then she took one boy under each arm and stepped out on the board again.

"Now you're really going to have some fun," she said. "It's almost like walking the tight rope."

When she got to the middle of the board she lifted one leg in the air just as she had done at the circus. The crowd below gasped, and when a little later Pippi lost one of her shoes several old ladies fainted. However, Pippi reached the tree safely with the little boys. Then the crowd cheered so loudly that the dark night was filled with noise and the sound drowned out the crackling of the fire.

Pippi hauled up the rope, fastened one end securely to a branch and tied the other around one of the boys. Then she let him down slowly and carefully into the arms of his waiting mother, who was beside herself with joy when she had him safe. She held him close and hugged him, with tears in her eyes.

But Pippi yelled, "Untie the rope, for goodness' sake! There's another kid up here, and he can't fly either."

So the people helped to untie the rope and free the little boy. Pippi could tie good knots, she could indeed. She had learned that at sea. She pulled up the rope again, and now it was the second boy's turn to be let down.

Pippi was alone in the tree. She sprang out on the board, and all the people looked at her and wondered what she was going to do. She danced back and forth on the narrow board. She raised and lowered her arms gracefully and sang in a hoarse voice that could barely be heard down in the square:

> "*The fire is burning,*
> *It's burning so bright,*
> *The flames are leaping and prancing.*

It's burning for you,
It's burning for me,
It's burning for all who are dancing!"

As she sang she danced more and more wildly until many people covered their eyes in horror for they were sure she would fall down and kill herself. Flames came leaping out of the gable window, and in the firelight people could see Pippi plainly. She raised her arms to the night sky, and while a shower of sparks fell over her she cried loudly, "Such a jolly, jolly fire!"

She took one leap and caught the rope. "Look out!" she cried and came sliding down the rope like greased lightning.

"Three cheers for Pippi Longstocking! Long may she live!" cried the fire chief.

"Hip, hip, hurray! Hip, hip, hurray! Hip, hip, hurray!" cried all the people—three times. But there was one person there who cheered four times.

It was Pippi Longstocking.

11

Pippi Celebrates Her Birthday

O NE day Tommy and Annika found a letter in their mailbox.

It was addressed to TMMY and ANIKA, and when they opened it they found a card which read:

TMMY AND ANIKA ARE INVITED TO PIPPI'S
TOMORO TO HER BERTHDAY PARTY. DRES:
WARE WATEVER YOU LIK.

Tommy and Annika were so happy they began to skip and dance. They understood perfectly well what was printed on the card although the spelling was a little unusual. Pippi had had a great deal of trouble writing it. To be sure, she had not recognized the letter "i" in school the day she was there,

but all the same she could write a little. When she
was sailing on the ocean one of the sailors on her
father's ship used to take her up on deck in the
evening now and then and try to teach her to write.
Unfortunately Pippi was not a very patient pupil.
All of a sudden she would say, "No, Fridolf"— that
was his name—"no, Fridolf, bother all this learning! I can't study any more now because I must
climb the mast to see what kind of weather we're
going to have tomorrow."

So it was no wonder the writing didn't go so well
now. One whole night she sat struggling with that
invitation, and at dawn, just as the stars were paling
in the sky over Villa Villekulla, she tiptoed over to
Tommy's and Annika's house and dropped the letter into their mailbox.

As soon as Tommy and Annika came home from
school they began to get all dressed up for the
party. Annika asked her mother to curl her hair, and
her mother did, and tied it with a big pink satin
bow. Tommy combed his hair with water so that it
would lie all nice and smooth. He certainly didn't
want any curls. Then Annika wanted to put on her
very best dress, but her mother thought she'd better
not for she was seldom neat and clean when she came

home from Pippi's; so Annika had to be satisfied with her next best dress. Tommy didn't care what suit he wore so long as he looked nice.

Of course they had bought a present for Pippi. They had taken the money out of their own piggy banks, and on the way home from school had run into the toy shop on Main Street and bought a very beautiful—well, what they had bought was a secret for the time being. There it lay, wrapped in green paper and tied with a great deal of string, and when they were ready Tommy took the package, and off they went, followed by their mother's warning to take good care of their clothes. Annika was to carry the package part of the way, and they were both to hold it when they handed it to Pippi—that they had agreed upon.

It was already November, and dusk came early. When Tommy and Annika went in through the gate of Villa Villekulla they held each other's hands tightly, because it was quite dark in Pippi's garden and the wind sighed mournfully through the bare old trees. "Seems like fall," said Tommy. It was so much pleasanter to see the lighted windows in Villa Villekulla and to know that they were going to a birthday party.

Ordinarily Tommy and Annika rushed in through the kitchen door, but this time they went to the front door. The horse was not on the porch. Tommy gave a lively knock on the door.

From inside came a low voice:

> *"Who comes in the dark night*
> *On the road to my house?*
> *Is it a ghost or just*
> *A poor little mouse?"*

"No, no, Pippi, it's us," shrieked Annika. "Open the door!"

Pippi opened the door.

"Oh, Pippi, why did you say that about a ghost? I was so scared," said Annika and completely forgot to congratulate Pippi.

Pippi laughed heartily and opened the door to the kitchen. How good it was to come in where it was light and warm! The birthday party was to be in the kitchen, because that was the pleasantest room in the house. There were only two other rooms on the first floor, the parlor in which there was only one piece of furniture and Pippi's bedroom. The kitchen was large and roomy, and Pippi had

scrubbed it until it shone. She had put rugs on the
floor and a large new cloth on the table. She had
embroidered the cloth herself with flowers that certainly looked most remarkable, but Pippi declared
that such flowers grew in Farthest India, so of
course that made them all right. The curtains were
drawn and the fire burned merrily. On the woodbox
sat Mr. Nilsson, banging pot lids together. In a
corner stood the horse, for he too had been invited
to the party.

Now at last Tommy and Annika remembered that
they were supposed to congratulate Pippi. Tommy
bowed and Annika curtsied and then they handed
Pippi the green package and said, "May we congratulate you and wish you a happy birthday?"
Pippi thanked them and eagerly tore the package
open. And there was a music box! Pippi was wild
with delight. She patted Tommy and she patted
Annika and she patted the music box and she patted the wrapping paper. She wound up the music
box, and with much plinking and plonking out came
a melody that was probably supposed to be "Ack,
du käre Augustin."

Pippi wound and wound and seemed to forget
everything else. But suddenly she remembered

something. "Oh, my goodness, you must have your birthday presents too!" she said.

"But it isn't our birthday," said Tommy and Annika.

Pippi stared at them in amazement. "No, but it's my birthday, isn't it? And so I can give birthday presents too, can't I? Or does it say in your schoolbooks that such a thing can't be done? Is it something to do with that old pluttifikation that makes it impossible?"

"Oh, of course it's possible," said Tommy. "It just isn't customary. But for my part, I'd be very glad to have a present."

"Me too," said Annika.

Pippi ran into the parlor and brought back two packages from the chest. When Tommy opened his he found a little ivory flute, and in Annika's package was a lovely brooch shaped like a butterfly. The wings of the butterfly were set with blue and red and green stones.

When they had all had their birthday presents it was time to sit down at the table, where there were all sorts of cakes and buns. The cakes were rather peculiar in shape, but Pippi declared they were just the kind of cakes they had in China.

Pippi served hot chocolate with whipped cream, and the children were just about to begin their feast when Tommy said, "When Mamma and Papa have a party the gentlemen always get cards telling them what ladies to take in to dinner. I should think we ought to have cards too."

"Okay," said Pippi.

"Although it will be kind of hard for us because I'm the only gentleman here," added Tommy doubtfully.

"Fiddlesticks," said Pippi. "Do you think Mr. Nilsson is a lady, maybe?"

"Oh, of course not, I forgot Mr. Nilsson," said Tommy, and he sat down on the woodbox and wrote on a card:

"Mr. Settergren will have the pleasure of taking Miss Longstocking in to dinner."

"Mr. Settergren, that's me," said he with satisfaction and showed Pippi the card. Then he wrote on the next card:

"Mr. Nilsson will have the pleasure of taking Miss Settergren in to dinner."

"Okay, but the horse must have a card too," said Pippi decidedly, "even if he can't sit at the table." So Tommy, at Pippi's dictation, wrote:

"The horse will have the pleasure of remaining in the corner where he will be served cakes and sugar."

Pippi held the card under the horse's nose and said, "Read this and see what you think of it."

As the horse had no objection to make, Tommy offered Pippi his arm, and they walked to the table. Mr. Nilsson showed no intention of offering his arm to Annika, so she took a firm hold of him and lifted him up to the table. But he didn't want to sit on a chair; he insisted on sitting right on the table. Nor did he want any chocolate with whipped cream, but when Pippi poured water in his cup he took it in both his hands and drank.

Annika and Tommy and Pippi ate and ate, and Annika said that if these cakes were the kind they had in China then she intended to move to China when she grew up.

When Mr. Nilsson had emptied his cup he turned it upside down and put it on his head. When Pippi saw that, she did the same, but as she had not drunk quite all her chocolate a little stream ran down her forehead and over her nose. She caught it with her tongue and lapped it all up.

"Waste not, want not," she said.

Tommy and Annika licked their cups clean before they put them on their heads.

When everybody had had enough and the horse had had his share, Pippi took hold of all four corners of the tablecloth and lifted it up so that the cups and plates tumbled over each other as if they were in a sack. Then she stuffed the whole bundle in the wood-box.

"I always like to tidy up a little as soon as I have eaten," she said.

Then it was time for games. Pippi suggested that they play a game called "Don't touch the floor." It was very simple. The only thing one had to do was walk all around the kitchen without once stepping on the floor. Pippi skipped around in the twinkling of an eye, and even for Tommy and Annika it was quite easy. You began on the drainboard, and if you stretched your legs enough it was possible to step onto the back of the stove. From the stove to the woodbox, and from the woodbox to the hat shelf,

and down onto the table, and from there across two
chairs to the corner cupboard. Between the corner
cupboard and the drainboard was a distance of several feet, but, luckily, there stood the horse, and if
you climbed up on him at the tail end and slid off at
the head end, making a quick turn at exactly the
right moment, you landed exactly on the drainboard.

When they had played this game for a while and
Annika's dress was no longer her next-best dress but
her next-next-next-best one, and Tommy had become as black as a chimney sweep, then they decided
to think up something else.

"Suppose we go up in the attic and visit the
ghosts," suggested Pippi.

Annika gasped. "A-a-are there really ghosts in
the attic?" she asked.

"Are there ghosts? Millions!" said Pippi. "It's
just swarming with all sorts of ghosts and spirits.
You trip over them wherever you walk. Shall we go
up?"

"Oh, Pippi!" said Annika and looked reproachfully at her.

"Mamma says there aren't any such things as
ghosts and goblins," said Tommy boldly.

"And well she might," said Pippi, "because there aren't any anywhere else. All the ghosts in the world live in my attic. And it doesn't pay to try to make them move. But they aren't dangerous. They just pinch you in the arm so you get black and blue, and they howl, and they play ninepins with their heads."

"Do—do—do they really play n-n-ninepins with their heads?"

"Sure, that's just what they do," said Pippi. "Come on, let's go up and talk with them. I'm good at playing n-n-ninepins."

Tommy didn't want to show that he was frightened, and in a way he really did want to see a ghost. That would be something to tell the boys at school! Besides, he consoled himself with the thought that the ghosts probably wouldn't dare to hurt Pippi. He decided to go along. Poor Annika didn't want to go under any circumstances, but then she happened to think that a little tiny ghost might sneak downstairs while she was sitting alone in the kitchen. That decided the matter. Better to be with Pippi and Tommy among thousands of ghosts than alone in the kitchen with even the tiniest little ghost child.

Pippi went first. She opened the door to the attic stairs. It was pitch-dark there. Tommy took a firm grip on Pippi, and Annika took an even firmer grip on Tommy, and so they went up. The stairs creaked and squeaked with every step. Tommy began to wonder if it wouldn't have been better to stay down in the kitchen, and Annika didn't need to wonder— she was sure of it. At last they came to the top of the stairs and stood in the attic. It was pitch-dark there too, except where a little moonbeam shone on the floor. There were sighs and mysterious noises in every corner when the wind blew in through the cracks.

"Hi, all you ghosts!" shrieked Pippi.

But if there was any ghost there he certainly didn't answer.

"Well, I might have known," said Pippi, "they've gone to a council meeting of the Ghost and Goblin Society."

Annika sighed with relief and hoped that the meeting would last a long time. But just then an awful sound came from one of the corners of the attic.

"Whoo-ooo-ooo!" it said, and a moment later Tommy saw something come rushing toward him in the dimness. He felt it brush his forehead and saw something disappear through a little window that stood open.

He shrieked to high heaven, "A ghost! A ghost!"

And Annika shrieked with him.

"That poor thing will be late for the meeting," said Pippi. "If it was a ghost. And not an owl. For that matter, there aren't any ghosts," she continued after a while. "If anybody insists that there are ghosts, I'll tweak him in the nose."

"Yes, but you said so yourself," said Annika.

"Is that so? Did I?" said Pippi. "Well, then I'll certainly tweak my own nose."

And she took a firm grip on her nose and tweaked it.

After that Tommy and Annika felt a little calmer. In fact they were now so courageous that they ventured to go up to the window and look out over the garden. Big dark clouds sailed through the sky and did their best to hide the moon. And the wind sighed in the trees.

Tommy and Annika turned around. But then— oh, horrors—they saw a white figure coming toward them.

"A ghost!" shrieked Tommy wildly.

Annika was so scared she couldn't even shriek. The ghost came nearer and nearer. Tommy and Annika hugged each other and shut their eyes.

But then they heard the ghost say, "Look what I found! Papa's nightshirt in an old sea chest over here. If I hem it up around the bottom I can wear it."

Pippi came up to them with the nightshirt dangling around her legs.

"Oh, Pippi, I could have died of fright," said Annika.

"But nightshirts aren't dangerous," Pippi assured her. "They don't bite anybody except in self-defense."

Pippi now decided to examine the sea chest thoroughly. She lifted it up and carried it over to the window and opened the cover, so that what little moonlight there was fell on the contents of the chest. There were a great many old clothes, which she threw out on the attic floor. There were a telescope, a few books, three pistols, a sword, and a bag of goldpieces.

"Tiddelipom and piddeliday," said Pippi contentedly.

"It's so exciting!" said Tommy.

Pippi gathered everything in the nightshirt,

and down they went into the kitchen again. Annika was perfectly satisfied to leave the attic.

"Never let children handle firearms," said Pippi and took a pistol in each hand and prepared to fire. "Otherwise some accident can easily happen," she said, shooting off both pistols at once. "That was a good bang," she announced and looked up in the ceiling. The bullets had made two holes.

"Who knows?" she said hopefully. "Perhaps the bullets have gone right through the ceiling and hit some ghosts in the legs. That will teach them to think twice before they set out to scare any innocent little children again. Because even if there aren't any ghosts, they don't need to go round scaring folks out of their wits, I should think. Would you each like a pistol?" she asked.

Tommy was enchanted, and Annika also very much wanted a pistol, provided it wasn't loaded.

"Now we can organize a robber band if we want to," said Pippi. She held the telescope up to her eyes. "With this I can almost see the fleas in South America, I think," she continued. "And it'll be good to have if we do organize a robber band."

Just then there was a knock at the door. It was Tommy's and Annika's father, who had come to take them home. It was long past their bedtime, he said. Tommy and Annika hurried to say thank you, bid Pippi good-by, and collect all their belongings, the flute, the brooch, and the pistols.

Pippi followed her guests out to the porch and watched them disappear through the garden. They turned around to wave. The light from inside shone on her. There she stood with her stiff red braids, dressed in her father's nightshirt which billowed around her feet. In one hand she held a pistol and in the other the sword. She saluted with it.

When Tommy and Annika and their father reached the gate they heard her calling. They stopped to listen. The wind whistled through the trees so they could just barely hear what she said.

"I'm going to be a pirate when I grow up," she cried. "Are you?"